He could not shake the feeling something was wrong or deny his desire to try to get her to open up.

"See you tomorrow," she said, still holding on to her pack.

"It shouldn't take me long," he said. "I'll be back before noon."

"Noon," she repeated as though committing it to memory.

"Yes. Well, good night," he said, and damn if he didn't feel a pull toward touching her lips with his, and double damn if she didn't seem to broadcast the hope he would do just that.

They both stepped back at the same time. As he walked down the short hallway back to the kitchen, he heard the door close and the lock click behind him.

He'd never been around a woman who sent so many mixed messages. Messages he was desperate to explore.

COWBOY CAVALRY

ALICE SHARPE

This book is dedicated to my family, who make
everything worth doing. I love you all.

Recycling programs
for this product may
not exist in your area.

ISBN-13: 978-0-373-74990-4

Cowboy Cavalry

Copyright © 2016 by Alice Sharpe

Printed in U.S.A.

www.Harlequin.com

Alice Sharpe met her husband-to-be on a cold, foggy beach in Northern California. Their union has survived the rearing of two children, a handful of earthquakes, numerous cats and a few special dogs. Alice and her husband now live near Portland, Oregon, where she devotes the majority of her time to pursuing her second love, writing. Please visit her at www.alicesharpe.com for information about upcoming titles.

Books by Alice Sharpe

Harlequin Intrigue

The Brothers of Hastings Ridge Ranch

Cowboy Incognito
Cowboy Undercover
Cowboy Secrets
Cowboy Cavalry

The Rescuers

Shattered
Stranded

The Legacy

Undercover Memories
Montana Refuge
Soldier's Redemption

Open Sky Ranch

Westin's Wyoming
Westin's Legacy
Westin Family Ties

Visit the Author Profile page at Harlequin.com for more titles.

CAST OF CHARACTERS

Frankie Hastings—The youngest of the Hastings brothers, Frankie has been living with secrets his whole life—not only his but his mother's unrevealed past, as well. A run-in with an enigmatic beauty fuels his desire to take back his future. Now the goal becomes making sure they both survive to see it.

Kate West—She's desperately trying to keep her ailing grandmother afloat. When an opportunity to ensure security arises, she vows she'll take it no matter the cost to her peace of mind; she doesn't count on the cost to her heart.

Dave Dalton—He has something he wants to talk to Frankie about, something that could change everything. Is it true a dead man can't tell tales?

Gary Dodge—A producer intent on helping Frankie realize his dream to film a documentary about a one-hundred-year-old event. Is that his only intention?

Jay Thurman—He represents a part of Frankie's past that Frankie has tried to overcome. He's back now, meaner than ever, more determined to get "what's his," and he doesn't care who he has to destroy to do it.

Patrick Lowell—The documentary team's fuddy-duddy historian is positive there's gold buried on Hastings land. If he's right, its discovery will make a heck of an ending for the film.

Ed Hoskins—Does this numismatist hold the key Frankie needs to unlock the deadly mystery of his past?

Gerard, Chance and Pike Hastings—Frankie's brothers swear to stand—or fall—together.

Sara Kane—This grieving daughter has a hundred thousand reasons to support her conviction that her father did not commit suicide.

Chapter One

Kate took a seat at an outdoor waterfront table and settled back to wait. She was purposefully early, wanting time to catch her breath, to go over what she would say and how. Normal life as of late afforded few opportunities for introspection and as she closed her eyes and turned her face to the sun, she realized she was a little rusty when it came to intrigue.

No matter. She may have grown up here in Seattle, but she'd spent the last eight years in Arizona and appreciated the rare May warmth currently caressing her skin. When was the last time she'd been free to just sit for a few moments without distraction? She couldn't remember, and even now, the urge to get back prevented her from fully living in this moment.

"Kate West?" a male voice inquired and she opened her eyes with a start. She glanced up to find a man of about thirty staring down at her.

Sun-streaked brown hair combed away from his forehead framed bluish gray eyes that echoed the water sparkling behind him.

"Yes, I'm Kate," she said.

"I knew it." His smile was dazzling as he offered his hand. "Gary Dodge told me to look for a stunning blonde."

"You must be Frank Hastings," she said, suppressing laughter and an eye roll. She was well aware she looked dog-tired, worn-out and frazzled.

"Please, call me Frankie," he said as he released her fingers. "May I sit down?"

She nodded and watched as he took a seat across from her. She'd seen his picture so she'd known he was attractive, but the photograph hadn't caught the energy pulsing through his body. It also hadn't caught the lively curiosity behind his eyes. Her confidence in her ability to stay one step ahead of him took a nosedive as he returned her gaze with open appraisal.

She knew that along with his father and brothers he ran a huge ranch in Central Idaho. Assumedly, he had picked up the golden tan of his skin the honest way, by being outside but there was also something decidedly uncowboylike about him, too, and that was interesting.

He smiled again as though aware she was sizing him up. The whites of his eyes and teeth almost glowed in his face and she found herself comparing him to her ex. She looked down at her hands immediately. Thinking about an ex-boyfriend wasn't going to get her anywhere. She warned herself to concentrate on her grandmother.

"Is something wrong?" he asked.

She ran fingers across her brow and shook her head. "No."

"Thank you for agreeing to meet me," he added as a waiter showed up. He ordered crab cakes and a salad, without glancing at the menu. She ordered iced tea and nothing else. "I've heard about your…issue with our project," he added after the waiter left. "I'm anxious to set your mind at ease."

"Are you?"

"Yes, of course. Why do you say it like that?"

"It seems kind of hopeless," she said. "Gary, your producer, has already tried to convince me how wrong I am. I'm afraid you drove all the way here from Idaho for nothing."

His eyes narrowed a hair. "Just give me a chance," he said as her tea and a basket of bread appeared on their table.

"Listen," she said, tearing off a hunk of sourdough, hoping it would settle her stomach. Darn nerves. "I understand that my eleventh-hour objections to this movie—"

"Not a movie," he said. "A documentary."

"What's the difference?"

He shrugged. "Pretty vast. A movie can be pure fiction or a takeoff on known facts. Either way, liberties are taken. A documentary sticks to the truth, not conjectures."

"Truth as interpreted through a human lens," she said.

"You mean the angle the director decides to emphasize?"

"Yes."

"That's true, but this is all pretty cut-and-dried stuff. One hundred years ago, four men robbed the bank in what was once known as Green Ridge, Idaho. That's a fact. Two days later, three of them were caught by a posse—Samuel and Earl Bates and a guy called William Adler. They were taken back to the big oak tree two miles outside town and hung. That's a sad fact, but a fact nonetheless. The fourth man got away. It's generally assumed he took all the gold with him.

"The robbery more or less killed Green Ridge, though in all truth, the mine was close to playing out. A few years after the town emptied, a new generation of gold diggers found a small vein, but nothing more. All that remains now is a dead mine and a ghost town both of which are on our land, practically in our backyard. And the hanging tree, of course. Our historian has found two descendants of men who might be the elusive fourth man. I spoke to one of them last week and he said he had something pretty special to show me. It's an exciting time."

She'd chewed on her chunk of bread while he spoke. It wasn't helping her nerves at all. She already knew everything he'd told her and she was certain he knew what she was about to say, too. Gary Dodge would have told him. She said it anyway.

"What you have to remember," she began, "is that my great-great-great-grandfather Earl Bates and his brother, Samuel, were two of the men killed by that vigilante posse. It's well-known they received no trial and there was no hard evidence against them. They may have been innocent—they certainly deserved better justice than hysterical murderers taking the law into their own hands. I couldn't live with myself if I didn't try to keep you guys from glorifying their killers."

"We have no desire to glorify anyone or anything," Frankie said, and for the first time, his voice reflected irritation. She knew that both Frankie and Gary Dodge had worked on this project for over a year. It was important to them. Seeing Frankie's less polished side made dealing with him both easier and more difficult for her: easier because his feelings were involved and who better than she knew how that could warp a person's judgment? Harder, because she could feel his enthusiasm and that made him a little irresistible.

"Maybe not," she protested, "but it's not too difficult to imagine that's exactly what will happen. I'm the last of my family. For decades, Samuel and Earl have just been footnotes no one really cared about. Your project has the potential to change that."

"And perhaps give meaning to their deaths," Frankie said suddenly as though he'd just thought of this angle. They were both silent as his meal was delivered. It looked delicious, but Kate didn't think she could have eaten it even if she could afford to buy it.

Frankie ignored his plate. He sat forward. "You've brought up some interesting facts. I'll make sure they're addressed."

Now you're just being glib, she thought as she shook her head. "No," she said. "The truth is I have an appointment to meet with your backers very soon. If they don't walk away, I'll keep talking until somebody listens."

Frankie stared at her for a minute. It was obvious his mind was racing. She could almost picture him running along a hall, throwing open door after door, looking for the right response that would get her to change her mind. She'd expected this from him—she'd been warned that he was formidable when thwarted.

"Okay, here's the thing, Kate," he said at last. "You're young and smart and articulate and maybe worse, from our point of view, you're very pretty. Social media will love you. You may not have a lot of legal ground to stand on when it comes to stopping us, but you could do damage with negative publicity. More than that, though, our backers are a cautious lot. They're going to come to the same conclusions I have when they meet you and I'm afraid they'll get cold feet. This matters too much to me to risk that. What can I do or say to change your mind?"

"Nothing," she insisted.

"There has to be something."

"No," she said. "There doesn't. I tried to warn you."

He took a breath. "Please, can't you just be reasonable?"

"You're calling me unreasonable?"

His jaw tightened. "You've brought up interesting points, I admit that, but they can be dealt with fairly. We work with a dedicated researcher, a historian, who checks all our facts. We aren't interested in rewriting history. Can you say the same?"

She put down her fork. This guy was conceited or was that her guilty conscience making excuses for her own motivation? She picked up her tea glass and took a sip, giving herself a chance to calm down, check her watch and take a deep breath. "I understand that making this documentary is important to you," she said. "You grew up with this story, you live close to where it all happened—it's intimate to you in a way it isn't for me. This is all I can do to honor the memories of the men who died without the opportunity to defend themselves."

"Believe it or not, I have empathy for the men who were hung. It was a gruesome way to die. Can't you find it in your heart to trust me with their story?"

"I sense you mean well," she said carefully, "but I don't know what the rest of your family is like and according to Mr. Dodge, they play a big part in this thing."

He steepled his fingers and gazed at her. "I have an idea," he said at last.

"What is it?"

"Come to Idaho. Meet my father and brothers, and Grace, my stepmother. You'll love her, everyone does."

"Your father," she said slowly. "What kind of man is he?"

Frankie appeared surprised by her question. Maybe she shouldn't have asked it.

"A decent man," he said. "A man who puts his family first."

"Family first," she mumbled. "Over everything?"

"What do you mean?"

"Over his land, for instance? Over money?"

Frankie's brow wrinkled. "I'm sorry, Kate. I'm not sure what you're getting at."

"It doesn't matter," she said, and straightened her shoulders, figuratively if not literally. "How many brothers do you have?"

"Three. All older." He sat back. "None of us have a secret agenda of any kind. We just want the past recorded in a fair and honest way. This story has always fascinated me. Come meet everyone. Come get to know the countryside where this happened, walk the dead streets of a once vibrant town, get a feel for the folks who lived and loved there, understand their struggles and that includes your own relatives. In other words, come back to Idaho with me."

"Now?" she said. "Just like that?"

"Yes."

She stared at him. Would this be easier if he wasn't so good-looking? Maybe.

"As a matter of fact," he added, as though sweetening the deal, "on my way home I'm stopping to meet with one of the descendants I told you about. You're welcome to come along and meet him, too."

"Why would I want to do that?"

"Just to get a feel for our approach. The man I'm talking to is the great-great-grandson of a guy named Matthew Dalton. Dalton was a lawyer in Green Ridge. He married a woman named Mary two days after the robbery and they left town the day after that. Accounts hint it was all very sudden. Maybe he was the fourth man, who knows? Hopefully we'll learn something that can help us piece together the truth. Will you give me a chance, say a week or so to try to awaken a little curiosity in you?"

"I don't know," she said softly.

"If it's your job—"

"I… I work at home," she said quickly. "There are arrangements that would have to be made, of course, but it's not that. My car is kind of on its last legs…"

"You can ride with me."

"It's not the getting there that worries me," she said. "I just don't know how comfortable I'd feel on your turf."

"Well, you can leave whenever you want, of course." He shook his head and added, "I didn't even think. Is there someone you'd like to have come with you? A family member, a friend?"

"No," she said and quickly averted her gaze. Luke had once told her he could read her mind just by staring into her eyes.

When still she hesitated, he lowered his voice. "Just so you know, one of my brothers is married and expecting a baby any second, another is getting married this summer and Pike's girlfriend is due for a visit at the end of the week. She's a private investigator in New York. In other words, there are lots of women around so if you're worried about being stuck with a bunch of guys, don't be."

"I'm not worried about being with men," she said.

He flashed her a devil-may-care smile. "Really? Now that's…interesting."

In that moment, Luke's memory pierced her heart like a poison dart. He'd had this same throw-caution-to-the-wind-and-say-whatever-he-was-thinking quality.

"Sorry, I was just joking around," he added quickly. "Thought I'd lighten things up."

"I know. It's okay."

"Please say you'll give my suggestion some thought."

She glanced at his uneaten food as her mind raced, then she glanced at her watch. She'd been away almost two hours!

"If you'd rather travel on your own," he said,

"that's fine, too. We'll pay for you to rent a car or buy you a ticket. Just promise you'll keep an open mind."

"No matter what you think of me, I am capable of being fair," she said.

"Good."

She nodded once. "Okay, I'll come. I'll meet everyone and look around, all of that. But you and Mr. Dodge have to understand that none of it may change my mind and I expect both of you to respect that I have a right to my opinion."

"I get it," he said. "And I appreciate your honesty."

"Under the circumstances, I'll take the rented car."

"Fine. If you trust me to do it for you, I'll make the arrangements and have it delivered to your house later today. Let me jot down directions to our ranch," he added. "Or give me your email address and I'll send them to you."

"That won't be necessary. Let's say we meet at the Hertz car rental place at the airport tomorrow morning at nine. I'll follow you to your interview and then on to your ranch."

"That sounds great," he said. "And, Kate, thank you for giving us this chance."

"Just remember that's all it is," she said softly, meeting his gaze straight on, bracing herself for the intensity in his eyes. "A chance."

Chapter Two

Frankie was almost positive there was more to Kate West than met the eye, although there was nothing at all wrong with what met the eye. Midtwenties, long spun-gold hair, forget-me-not blue eyes, skin like polished seashells.

But there was something else, too. How many times had she looked at her watch for instance? Gary hadn't said a word about her being distracted when he met her. Did that mean she normally wasn't or had Gary been too engrossed in preproduction dilemmas to notice?

She'd contacted Gary first. He'd immediately called their historian, Patrick Lowell, to make sure she was legitimate. Pat was a fuddy-duddy of a man, a former junior college teacher turned freelance researcher, hired by Gary for several projects through the years and thorough with dates and facts. He'd confirmed Kate's claims. Gary called Frankie who left the ranch in Falls

Bluff and drove all night to meet with Gary and Pat.

Pat had admitted he didn't know much about Kate's current situation, just that she'd once been a grammar schoolteacher in Arizona. He'd suggested Frankie invite her to the ranch so she could meet the family. Gary had seconded that idea. Obviously, they both thought Frankie's family would be more successful at winning her over than Frankie would.

But Frankie had settled on lunch instead and he'd gone to the restaurant dead set against inviting her anywhere. Once she'd met everyone, then what? What in the world would he do with a stranger intent on causing him problems? It was a busy time of year and taking care of her would fall on his shoulders. He really didn't like babysitting people. Left to his own devices, he would have invited her to do her best to convince the world the documentary didn't deserve to be made and he'd do his best to prove her wrong by making sure it turned out so damn good, there could be no doubt.

But he wasn't in this by himself; Gary was involved, too, and so when Kate unconsciously laid the groundwork for an invitation, he went ahead and made it. The truth was that getting to know her was not an unpleasant idea. Who didn't like a little mystery in a woman? He was even a bit disappointed that she wanted to drive separately.

But first he wanted to know what she was hiding and that's why he'd paid for lunch and left the restaurant before her, which wasn't easy as she was obviously champing at the bit to be gone herself.

Why? Had she privately arranged to talk to the backers earlier than she'd claimed? Had she agreed to the ranch trip just to mislead him? He intended to find out, even if it meant he had to sneak around a little.

From the restaurant exit, he glanced back at their table to see the waiter boxing his untouched lunch. Waste not, want not, huh? Maybe she had a dog. He hurried to his car and had just ducked inside when she stepped onto the sidewalk. She turned a fair number of heads as she walked down the block, blond hair floating out behind her in the gentle breeze, skirt swirling around excellent legs, small white paper bag dangling from one hand.

Babysitting her wasn't going to be that difficult, he admitted to himself. He just had to remember to treat her like a loaded keg of dynamite and not the living, breathing, sexy beauty that she was.

As she came to a halt at a nearby bus stop, her gaze darted between her wristwatch and the street until a bus passed Frankie's parked car and pulled to a stop in front of her. She boarded. He wasn't sure where it was bound because he'd been too busy admiring Kate's willowy form to notice the destination. He followed along behind as it made its way through traffic, expecting a downtown route. Instead it slowly made its way toward the suburbs and one of the many small communities surrounding Seattle proper. He continued following its stop-and-go route, watching as Kate made a couple of transfers, curious now despite the increasingly remote possibility her destination had anything to do with him. She finally got off the bus and began walking.

At first, the streets and sidewalks were crowded and all he had to do was drive slow and stay behind her. She kept making turns that led her away from the artsy-craftsy streets toward a row of ordinary houses, circa 1950. He stayed as far back as he could, her gold hair a beacon up ahead until she turned another corner and he sped up to find her again.

Many of the houses on this street were in the process of renovation but a few looked as though they hadn't been tinkered with for decades. He stopped as she opened the gate to one such house and walked across the barren yard. It appeared to him she knocked before unlocking the door with a key she took from her shoulder bag.

So, what had he learned? Not much. She apparently lived on a street showing signs of promise in a house whose property value undoubtedly superseded the worth of the structure.

As he sat there undecided about what to do next, the door opened again and a small older woman emerged wearing nothing but a baggy sleeveless dress. The door swung closed behind her as she walked across the yard and out through the gate, right into the middle of the street. She stopped suddenly and stared down at her bare feet, clutching her thin arms with her hands, her gaze traveling the block as though trying to place herself.

Frankie looked toward the door. No sign of Kate.

He pulled the car forward and got out. He stood there a second, kind of lurking behind a bush, willing Kate to come out and take care of this woman before he had to blow his cover and do it himself. The door stayed closed. A car came around the corner and started down the street and he knew it was time to act. He took off his jacket as he crossed to the woman and draped it over her shoulders. The car sped by them and Frankie suppressed a wave of anger lest the old woman thought it was directed at her.

"Can I help you?" he asked gently.

She didn't respond. He applied soft pressure to her arm to urge her to come with him back to the curb. She looked up at him as though just aware of his presence. "Do you know where Dennis is?"

"No, ma'am, I'm sorry, I don't," he said.

She looked down the street but didn't move.

Another car had pulled to a stop a few feet away and the impatient driver tapped the horn. The old lady jumped.

Frankie cast the driver a look that would have sent a pack of coyotes off at a run. "Ma'am, please," he said. "Come with me."

She peered at his face and blinked. "Do you know where Dennis is?"

"Gram!" Kate yelled from the yard. She tore open the gate and ran out into the street, glancing up at Frankie as she ground to a halt in front of him. To say she looked surprised to see him was an understatement. Shocked was more like it. The old woman gazed at Kate without changing expression. Kate's arm wrapped protectively around her shoulders. "Your dinner is almost ready, Gram," she said softly. "Let's go back inside. It's chilly out here."

"I can't find Dennis," the old lady mumbled.

"We'll look for him in the house," Kate promised as she led her grandmother back to the yard where Frankie now saw another woman waiting on the porch. Kate took Frankie's jacket from around her grandmother's shoulders, hooked it on the gate and glanced back at him, anger blazing in her eyes.

"Kate," he said but she shook her head and held up a hand as if to silence him. Without another word, she took her grandmother's arm and ushered her quickly inside the house, the other woman following behind. The door closed with a resounding thud.

Frankie, still in the middle of the street walked toward the car that had honked. The driver's window rolled open.

"You proud of yourself?" he asked the driver.

A narrow-faced man about his own age responded. "Just get off the damn street before I run you down!"

There had been a period in Frankie's life where he would have pulled this bozo out of his car and punched him square in the nose. The desire to do just that was still there but time had tempered him. He stepped toward the curb and the car sped by.

Frankie retrieved his jacket from the fence and stood there awhile, sure Kate would come back outside and demand an explanation although he wasn't sure what he could offer. The door stayed resolutely shut. She'd really meant that final shake of her head. He finally got back in his car and drove off toward the airport where he rented a room for the night.

Would Kate show up tomorrow? Doubtful bordering on hell, no. He didn't have her phone number. Of course, he could call Gary and get it, but then Gary would sense there was a problem…no thanks, he didn't want to start fielding questions, not yet anyway. Besides, part of him admitted he'd already intruded enough.

The older woman was obviously Kate's grandmother but who was Dennis? Did these people have something to do with Kate's desire to stop the filming of the documentary?

Why hadn't he quit following her when it was obvious she wasn't going to a business meeting? What had compelled him to know about her? Was he treating her like an adversary? That was fine if that was the case because she was an adversary, she'd chosen that role when she announced her intentions.

As he lay in bed that night, he knew that he had probably just sabotaged his own project and he swore under his breath. If Kate refused to talk to any of them again and went instead to the backers fueled by her anger with him, he didn't think he'd have the stomach to try to stop her.

"IS THERE ANYTHING I can get you before I leave?" Rose McFadden whispered from the doorway.

Kate glanced from her slumbering grand-mother to the retired nurse and shook her head. Her voice equally soft, she responded. "No thanks."

"I'm going home to pack a bag but I'll be back tomorrow morning bright and early, okay?"

"I don't know," Kate said. "I'm not sure—"

"Now, please, child, listen to me," Rose said, stepping into the room. "I'd hate to see you cancel your trip because of what happened today. Anyone can make a mistake and forget to lock the door after themselves."

"I never have before," Kate said. She'd been preoccupied when she got home, her mind processing the lunch with Frankie Hastings, reliving the conversation, wondering if she'd slipped up anywhere. And as a result, she hadn't re-locked the door and her grandmother had walked outside into the middle of the street. If Frankie hadn't been there who knows what would have happened?

"I'll be here like we arranged," Rose said. "I promised Mr. Abernathy I'd help you and your grandmother and I intend to keep my word. Try to get some sleep."

Kate sat in the darkened room for what

seemed like hours, the sound of her grandmother's breathing the only noise in the whole world. Today was the longest she'd been gone in a year. How could she leave again? What had she been thinking to agree to this?

List your choices, her subconscious demanded. Easy: zero.

She glanced from the stack of bills on the corner of the desk visible through the open doorway to the unframed window she was in the process of replacing here in the bedroom. The house needed new plumbing, the roof was forty years old and she suspected termites had had their way with the foundation. She was going under, not slowly, but fast.

When Kate's grandfather had died, Kate had cried for days. That was the last time she'd allowed herself tears. She didn't even cry for Luke because she was afraid if she started she'd never quit. But now she felt them swell in her eyes and roll down her cheeks and she seemed unable to stop them.

"Dennis?"

Kate's head jerked toward the bed where she found her grandmother staring up at her. "No, Gram, Grandpa isn't here right now. It's just me, Kate."

Gram blinked a couple of times as though trying to process Kate's words. She'd once had dark blue eyes like Kate's but as the fire inside her soul slowly fizzled away, it seemed her eye color followed suit. Kate hastily wiped at her cheeks, but her grandmother caught a tear on her finger and touched it to her own lips.

"Oh, Gram," Kate said. It had been two decades since Gram had done the exact same thing when Kate ran her bike into a mailbox and gave herself a black eye.

Kate scooted down on her chair until she could rest her head on Gram's pillow. The old woman grasped her hand and Kate started talking in a soft, unhurried voice. "A week ago, I met an old friend of yours named Greg Abernathy," she began. "He's been abroad for years but he recently moved back to Seattle and came to see you. He was so sad that Grandpa had… well, he got all choked up. And then he told me something.

"He and Grandpa were coworkers a long time ago. He remembered Grandpa telling him about a long distant uncle who was a diamond merchant. When this guy stopped during his travels, he would put his diamonds in the bank of whatever town he was staying in. Well, it turns out that this one time, the bank was robbed and the diamonds were taken along with the gold. He never made a claim on what he'd lost because he didn't want anyone to know what he did for a living.

"Now this is where fate takes a hand," she continued. "Mr. Abernathy and Grandpa shared an office at the college. When Mr. Abernathy left to teach overseas, he stored a whole lot of boxes of books and papers. When he got back to Seattle recently, he decided to clean out the storage and it was while he was doing this that he found a file of Grandpa's in with his things and in the file was a copy of a paper detailing where the diamonds had been hidden after the robbery. He came here to give the file to Grandpa and to ask if Grandpa had ever tried to recover them."

Kate lowered her voice. "Mr. Abernathy could see that we're...struggling. Those diamonds are yours now, and they could make all the difference in the world. It's not a fortune, but it's probably enough to get the house up to code so we can remortgage and get some of the bills paid. The trouble is, they're on the land of a greedy, possessive man. If he were to claim the diamonds as his own and take us to court—well, how could we pay for that and, anyway, by the time it was settled it would be too late for you... for us. I have to find them, Gram. Mr. Abernathy said he would go but he's old now and, besides, this is my obligation, not his. It's an opportunity and I can't think of anything else to do. Only thing is, it means I have to leave for a couple of days…"

Gram's hand had grown slack. Kate turned her head to find the older woman's eyes closed. Kate had a very strong premonition that if she left her grandmother's side it would be for the last time. Of course, she felt that way every time she left the house, every time she kissed her good-night. It was always goodbye.

"I don't know what to do," she whispered into the night.

FRANKIE ARRIVED AT the car rental place early armed with coffee and a sheaf of papers Gary had given him to look over. He'd give Kate an hour to stand him up and then he'd hit the road.

A female shape pushed off from where she'd been leaning against a fence and he recognized Kate's lovely face despite the huge sunglasses resting on her nose. As she approached, he reminded himself to close his mouth instead of gaping in shock. She'd come?

Why?

As he grabbed the door handle to get out of the vehicle and start the process of renting her a car, she opened the back door, shrugged off a backpack and set it on the seat where it clanked as it landed. A second later she slipped into the passenger seat.

Today she wore jeans and a black windbreaker. Her long, blond hair had been woven into a thick, loose braid that trailed down her back. She took off the sunglasses as she turned to face him. Dark smudges under her eyes were more pronounced than they'd been the day before.

"I can't believe you came," he heard himself say.

"Neither can I but I said I would so I did. Let's get something straight, though. My grandmother is none of your business."

"I—"

"You went behind my back. You asked me to trust you and then you—"

"Sneaked around," he interrupted. "I know. I'm sorry. I wish I could take it back—" The scowl on her face cut his words short. "Okay, I get it. Well, let's rent you a car and get on our way."

"There's no need now," she said. "I just didn't want you to know where I lived. I like my privacy."

"I sort of figured that," he said dryly.

"Let's just go."

"Sounds good to me," he said, and started the engine before she could change her mind.

Chapter Three

As the luxury car ate up the miles, Kate didn't have the slightest idea what to say to the man behind the wheel. He'd offered her his untouched coffee but she'd declined—she didn't drink coffee anymore. The nerves that had taken up residence when this situation began made almost everything taste like dirty dishwater and sit uncomfortably in her stomach.

He seemed as willing to let the miles pass in silence as she was but probably not for the same reasons. Yesterday, sitting outside with the breeze ruffling their hair and the sound of seagulls mingling with the chatter of other diners, Frankie's energy and charisma had been hard enough to handle but not as over-the-top scary as now.

She took a deep breath that didn't help as the subtle scent of his aftershave wafted into her nose. She was aware of his hands on the wheel, his long fingers almost graceful. Her hands looked more like work hands than his did and she squashed the urge to sit on them.

"You're very quiet," he said, glancing at her. His dark lashes coupled with his grayish eyes made his gaze so intense her cheeks felt hot. That's what a guilty conscience could do to a person.

"Just tired," she said and that was the truth. After deciding to scrap this adventure, she'd tackled that stack of bills and reality had settled once again on her shoulders. She needed money and quite a bit of it if she was to keep Gram safe. She couldn't afford to allow fear to rule her decisions. Premonitions were notoriously overrated. She'd be back in two days, tops.

She'd had to leave so early this morning to catch the bus to the airport that she hadn't been able to say goodbye to Gram. Rose would take care of her and goodbyes never lasted in Gram's memory for more than a few seconds anyway, but it added to the unease churning Kate's gut. She turned her face toward the window where her pal, Mr. Sun, warmed the glass. Her eyes drifted closed.

She woke with a start, heart racing. Where was Gram? Had she gotten through the door again? Full consciousness returned with a sucker punch and she took a deep breath as she scanned her surroundings. Frankie Hastings stared at her. He'd pulled up in front of a diner and Kate's stomach growled.

"We've been on the road for four hours," he said. "We're almost at Dave Dalton's place. He's the guy I told you about who's descended from the lawyer who left town after the robbery. I'm kind of hungry and it looks like we could get a sandwich here if that's okay with you. It isn't fancy, but it's convenient."

She sat up straight. Her mouth felt like it was stuffed with old socks. She blinked a couple of times. Her wallet held about forty dollars and that had to get her back home. What she needed most and could actually afford was a free glass of water.

"I meant to remind you," he added. "LOGO, that's the name of Gary Dodge's production company, intends to cover your expenses for this trip. That included the rental car that you didn't use but is still an option when you want to return to Seattle." He smiled at her and added, "And no, we're not trying to buy you. I don't imagine you come cheap."

She raised her eyebrows.

"I didn't mean it that way," he said, and for once, he looked ill at ease, which strangely made her feel better.

"I am thirsty," she said.

"Good. Let's give this place a try."

The diner turned out to be a far cry from the waterfront bistro of the day before. Kate ordered a grilled cheese sandwich and it actually seemed to sit okay in her stomach for once. Toward the end of the meal, Frankie took out his cell phone and studied it. "I'm reminding myself how to get to Dave Dalton's place," he explained.

"Do you know what it is he wants to show you?"

"Not a clue. I'm curious, of course,"

"Is he expecting me to be there, too? If it's awkward, I can sit outside in the sun or something."

"I doubt your being there will be an issue but no, he's not expecting you. I arranged this meeting about a week ago, before I knew you'd be...with me."

"Before I made trouble," she said.

"Yeah. Listen, as long as I have my phone out, why don't you give me your email and cell number? Phones don't always work out at the ranch, but—"

"I don't have email or a cell phone," she said.

He stared at her a second as though he couldn't believe what he'd just heard her say.

"I moved here from Arizona over a year ago," she added. She had to give him some explanation so she went with the truth. "My grandpar-

ents didn't have internet or the...inclination...
to install it. When my tablet died, I just, well,
people lived for generations without computers, right?"

"You sound like my father's kind of girl," he
said. "He's not big into them, either."

She did not want to be compared to his father. "I loved my computer. I mean, you can't
get through college nowadays without...well,
those days are long over. Now there are other
things to keep me busy."

"Like what?" he said.

She looked down at her hands and shrugged.
"You know, work."

"What kind of work do you do?"

She should have anticipated these questions.
They were the kind almost everyone asked, she
was just woefully out of practice fielding idle
curiosity. Not sure why she felt the need to take
the sting out of her words, she smiled. "Remember that whole I like my privacy thing?"

"Yes," he said. "Sorry."

She pushed herself away from the table and
they both stood up. "Thank you for the sandwich and the tea," she added. "I'm going to the
ladies' room. I'll be right back, I know you're
anxious to get going."

"I'll wait for you in the car," he said as he
stood. As she watched him walk to the cash

register, the strangest pang of longing came over her.

Now what was that all about?

DAVE DALTON LIVED down a tree-lined lane a mile or so outside Spokane, Washington. The road was rutted with parallel tracks. Kate had gripped the edges of her seat as Frankie did his best to stay in the ruts, but inevitably the tires found all the uneven spots. Dalton needed to grade his long, bumpy driveway.

Frankie's gut feeling that Kate was hiding something just wouldn't go away. Sure, she was touchy, but it had to be more than that. Touchy was understandable. She'd accepted an invitation from a virtual stranger who openly questioned her convictions. He was a little wary of her, too. But it was something more, like the way she avoided direct answers to simple questions, hiding behind the privacy thing. Still every once in a while, he caught an unguarded comment or look and it made him smile inside.

When had he last been serious about a woman? Almost a year, he realized with a start. She'd been a nurse at the urgent care center, pretty and fun-loving, full of hopes and dreams. He'd broken it off with her when she got too clingy and talk of her dreams became talk of "their" dreams, dreams he didn't share.

Right after that, he'd started building himself a very private home even his family didn't know about. Years before, his father had given each of his sons their choice of land on which to construct houses when and if they wanted. Frankie's oldest brother, Gerard, had chosen a river view parcel not far upstream from the main house. He and Kinsey lived in it and would soon be joined by their baby who was due momentarily.

Next in age came Chance. He'd built himself an A-frame. His fiancée's name was Lily and she and her small son lived on the ranch, too. Pike came next. He'd renovated a barn into a really cool house. His girlfriend, Sierra, split her time between the ranch and New York City.

Frankie knew he didn't quite fit into his family of overachievers. It was difficult being the youngest of four brothers, all with different mothers, all very capable ranchers and businessmen. His designated title as a kid had been the screwup. And now, between one thing and another, he just liked to keep part of his life to himself, hence his secret hideaway. Half the time when his family thought he was in town carousing or causing mischief, he was actually working on his place.

So, in short, he knew a thing or two about privacy and keeping secrets, but there was only one that made him break into a cold sweat every time he thought about it. With Kate, that seemed to happen constantly. She acted like she was under a lot of stress from a lot of directions and despite how prickly she could be, he felt for her.

But right now she was hanging on to her seat and staring straight ahead as a small house finally appeared in a clearing at the end of the private road. He pulled to a stop and heard her expel a long breath.

"You okay?"

"Just glad to have that road behind me."

"Don't forget we still have to get back to the highway."

"Let me enjoy walking around for a minute." They got out of the car and she took several breaths. Some of the color started to return to her cheeks as she gazed around them.

"It's quiet here," she said. "And warm." She unzipped her windbreaker and started to pull it over her head. As she raised her arms, her blouse rode up with the jacket and three inches of creamy, smooth, velvety skin appeared at the delicious curve of her waist. By the time she got the windbreaker off and tugged her clothes into place, he had looked away, alarmed at how enticing he found that tiny peek of her flesh.

The house had a small concrete slab for a front porch and a steeply pitched roof, probably because it snowed here in the winter. A trio of moldy, faded garden gnomes sat by the bushes in front of the window. Frankie knocked against the wooden door and they stood there waiting as insects droned in the tall grass.

"Are you sure he's expecting you?" Kate asked.

"I should have texted him to confirm things. Let's check and see if his car is here.

The detached garage shared the same shabby, spare construction as the house. A door that slid across a wide opening was slightly cracked. Frankie rolled it open enough that he could see a sleek white car so new it still had the dealer's advertisement where the license plate would eventually go.

"Wow," Kate said as she looked under his raised arm.

"Funny what people spend their money on, isn't it?" Frankie said. "The house looks like it's about to fall down while there's a seventy-five-thousand-dollar car sitting in the garage."

"Seventy-five thousand dollars," Kate said, whistling. "I repeat, wow."

"Well, he's probably here. Let's go knock again."

No one came to the door this time, either. Kate walked out onto the grass opposite the front window, approached the glass cautiously and peered inside.

"See anything?" Frankie called.

"Yeah. It looks like a…" She stopped talking as her hands flew to cover her mouth and she quickly backed away from the window almost stumbling over her own feet.

"Kate! What's wrong?" Frankie asked as he started to walk toward her.

"No, open the door. Hurry," she cried, casting him a wild-eyed look. "Open the door."

He turned back around and tried to twist the knob, then he rammed his shoulder against the door.

"Hurry!" Kate said.

Raising his leg, he kicked at the thing and this time the old wood creaked but it still didn't budge. He ran to Kate's side. "What is it?"

Her skin had drained of color. "A man," she said. He glanced at the windows but from that distance, all he saw were their reflections. "I think he's…he's dead," she mumbled.

Frankie grabbed one of the plaster garden gnomes and smashed it against the window. As glass shattered to the ground the foul odor of rotting flesh all but slammed him in the face. Kate turned her back to him, braced her hands on her knees and retched as he peered into the heavily shadowed room.

A small-framed man with sandy white hair hung from a rope attached to a rafter while an overturned stool occupied the floor under his dangling feet. From the smell and the appearance of his face, it was obvious he'd been there for quite a while.

Frankie moved to grasp Kate's shoulders as she heaved. He tried patting her back but he didn't say anything. What was there to say? When she had finished, she looked even more pallid than before. She accepted the clean handkerchief he offered her. "Thanks," she whispered. "I saw a faucet by the garage. I'm going to go wash out my mouth."

He took out his cell phone and dialed 911. What had Dave Dalton wanted to show him? It now seemed unlikely he'd ever know.

THEY SAT IN the car and waited for the sheriff's department and an ambulance to arrive. Kate breathed through her mouth. Even with the windows rolled up, she was almost positive she could still smell the rotting corpse of that poor man. Her empty stomach clenched.

The ambulance and the sheriff's cars came with sirens. Frankie and Kate answered a dozen questions that added almost no information that mattered one way or another. The deputy who entered the house came out looking almost as washed-out as Kate felt. He was about her age and she got the feeling this might be his first dead body.

"I can't believe old Dave killed himself like that. Sara is going to be real broken up by this."

"Sara?"

"His daughter."

"Then it is Dave Dalton in there," Frankie said.

"Yeah, though his own mother wouldn't recognize him now. No note or nothing, either. Shame you folks had to find him."

"Did he live alone?" Kate asked.

"Yeah. Has since Polly died 'bout five years back."

"I'd never really met the man," Frankie said. "In fact, I only talked to him one time and exchanged a couple of emails." He explained about the documentary and added, "He seemed interested in showing me something. It just seems odd that he'd kill himself before he could do it."

"What did he want to show you?"

"I have no idea."

"You never can tell what's going on in someone's head," the deputy said.

Two EMTs came out of the house rolling a body bag between them and loaded it into the ambulance. The deputy, Frankie and Kate watched with somber expressions.

"That's a nice car in the garage," Frankie said as the ambulance left the yard. He'd already retraced the actions they'd taken since arriving at the Dalton house.

"He's got himself a hell of an entertainment system and a kitchen that looks like one of them that's on a cooking show," the deputy said. "I had no idea he had that kind of loot." The deputy took off his hat, scratched his head and pulled it back on. "Dave's dad died a few years back," he added. "Dave retired about then. Maybe he inherited some money. He wasn't exactly the chatty type."

"I guess it's true," Frankie said softly. "It takes more than money to make a person happy."

The remark hit close to home for Kate who glanced down the twisting road as the ambulance's taillights disappeared from view.

Chapter Four

Several hours later when they stopped for gas, Frankie asked Kate if she was hungry and she shook her head. "I don't think I could eat. You go ahead, though."

"I don't have an appetite either," he said. "Listen, Kate, I'm very sorry that you were with me today and had to see all that. I wish I'd known what we were getting ourselves in for.

"How could you possibly have known?"

"If I'd called or texted him and he hadn't responded we wouldn't have stopped…"

"Don't beat yourself up on my account," she said. "The deputy mentioned Mr. Dalton had a daughter. It's better that we found his body than she did, right?"

"I guess so," he said.

"Anyway, I was with my grandfather when he died." Now why had she told him that? When she'd signed on for this venture, she'd sworn she wouldn't talk about herself, invite confidences or reveal personal information. She had never lied to anyone before in her life and Frankie was making doing so now very hard because…well, she didn't know why exactly, she just found herself wanting to tell him things. She muttered, "Death happens."

"But not usually like that," he said.

"No, you're right. Poor man."

Once back on the road, the fatigue Kate couldn't seem to shake came back and once again she fell asleep. When she woke up, it was dark outside and the dashboard clock said it was half past eleven.

She'd been dreaming about people. Luke had been in one of them but she wasn't sure in what way. The most vivid had been of her grandmother who had been baking. She'd offered Kate a taste of cookie batter from a long spoon. Kate had stared at her, tears running down her cheeks, mumbling over and over again, *Gram, you're like you used to be! You're okay.* And her grandmother had laughed. *Of course I'm okay.*

Kate swallowed a knot. "Where are we?" she asked as she glanced at Frankie.

"We just ran over the cattle guard that is the ranch's unofficial welcome mat. Did you have a nice snooze?"

"I think so," she said. "I'm sorry I keep falling asleep."

"It's no problem," he said. "When you live out this far, you get used to time alone behind a wheel."

She looked out the window. The waxing moon illuminated nothing but fields. Maybe there wasn't a whole lot else to see. They traveled a couple of miles down a dirt-and-gravel road before cresting a hill. Below, Kate saw a large house and a scattering of dark buildings, but her gaze went to the winding path of the river. Her heart jumped into her throat. The Bowline River...the real reason she was here. She tore her attention from that tantalizing U-bend and concentrated on the house instead lest Frankie sense the direction of her thoughts.

"That's my family's house," he said.

"Does everyone live there?"

"No. Gerard, Chance and Pike all built homes scattered about on ranch land."

"But not you?"

He shrugged. "The only people who live full-time in this house are my father and his wife, my brother Chance's fiancée, Lily, and her little boy, Charlie. They'll move out after the wedding. I've talked to Grace and she says you're welcome to stay with them."

"What about you?"

"I have a room at the house for when I'm here or once in a while I stay with Pike."

"Then you don't live on the ranch?"

He cast her a quick glance. Dashboard lights illuminated part of his face and the dazzling white of his eyes. "I like my privacy, too," he said.

"Touché," she muttered.

Three dogs greeted them when they got out of the car. They all had dark fur though two also sported patches of white. Though difficult to tell in the semidark of the night, one looked like a Labrador retriever and the others like some kind of shepherd mix. Kate hadn't had a dog since she was fifteen and she knelt to pat them and accept welcoming licks across the cheek. Frankie handed her the backpack. "What did you pack, rocks? This thing weighs a ton."

She'd meant to grab the pack herself and gotten distracted by the dogs. She didn't respond to his remark, just took the pack and moved off while he retrieved a small suitcase from his trunk.

As she approached the house, she heard the sound of moving water and unable to resist, walked along the path to a point where she could glimpse the moonlit river below. Its banks could be her salvation if she kept her mind on her priorities and goals.

"Kate?" Frankie said.

At the sound of his voice, she jumped about two inches into the air.

"It's beautiful, isn't it?" he asked, his voice soft.

"Huh? Oh, yes. It is," she said and hoped he couldn't hear her heart hammering in her chest.

"Do you like rivers?

"Why do you ask?" she said, startled.

She sensed as much as saw the rise and fall of his shoulders. "Oh, you know. Some people are into mountains and forests, others crave the desert sun, some like the water."

She thought of Luke and the icy Bering Sea. "I guess I appreciate different things in all of them," she said, looking up at his face. There was just enough light to see the curiosity at play in his eyes, curiosity she had no desire to arouse.

Or did she? When was the last time she'd felt as alive as right that moment? All day she'd been fighting a bone-weary fatigue except for the few hours spent in numb shock after discovering Dave Dalton's body. Now, however, she was wide awake and most of that was because of what this river signified if she accomplished what she'd agreed to try. But she also knew that some of the way she felt was because of Frankie's shoulder grazing her own.

Was she unconsciously soliciting his attention? Was this part of that urge she had to level with him? Why had this plan been so much easier in theory than it was turning out to be in reality? She stepped away from him, her backpack held in front of her chest like a shield. If he'd had X-ray vision what would he make of its contents?

"It's getting late," he said, touching her arm and sending a shiver straight to her spine. "Let's see if anyone is still awake."

She turned away from the river and from Frankie.

Tomorrow she'd get started. With any luck, she'd be gone by the day after.

And Frankie? He was an obstacle, yes, but he was also an illusion. There was no room for fantasy when a pack of hungry wolves howled at the door.

"YOU TWO MUST be exhausted," Harry Hastings said. His gaze traveled from Frankie to Kate. "Young lady, how are you holding up?" This demand was made in his usual take-no-prisoners style.

Beside him, Kate kind of bristled. Frankie had called his family after he spoke to the police to report the hanging death of Dave Dalton so they could alert Gary Dodge and Pat Lowell, but he hadn't told them that Kate required kid glove treatment.

"What do you mean?" she said.

"That horrible suicide, of course," he replied, reaching for her backpack. "Hell of a thing for a young woman to come across."

He was dressed in his pajamas and robe and explained that Grace was spending the night over at Kinsey and Gerard's place. The baby was technically overdue and Grace spent as much time over there as she did here.

Kate tightened her grip on her backpack. "I'm fine," she said. "Mr. Dalton's…death… was tragic, of course. I feel bad for his family."

"I've never understood suicide," he replied. "Anyway, let me take that pack for you. Grace fixed up the downstairs room…"

"No, thank you," she said firmly, her grip on her pack growing tighter. "I've got this."

He held up both hands and laughed.

"Sorry," she said and smothered a yawn. "It's been a long day."

"Of course," his father said. "Frankie, get our guest settled. I'm off to bed. I know you have your hands full," he added, "but I was hoping you'd have time to help me tomorrow morning. Pike and Chance rode out yesterday to the high pastures to check things out and they called to report seeing one of the mares with a brand-new foal. Not sure how she slipped by us, but I'd appreciate your bringing her and the baby closer to the ranch. They're out near Bywater, somewhere around Ten Cent Creek."

"No problem," Frankie said. He turned his attention to Kate and added, "Would you like to come along?"

"No thanks," she said quickly.

"Saving your riding legs for the ghost town and the…hanging tree?"

"It'll give me a chance to sleep in," she said after a moment.

He gave her a double take. All this woman did was sleep. Was she ill?

Harry Hastings wandered out of the kitchen and Frankie, careful not to even glance at Kate's backpack, led her down the hall to the open door of a modest room with twin beds.

"Is there anything else I can get you?" he asked.

"No, everything looks very nice."

He nodded as he gazed down in her eyes. He could not shake the feeling something was wrong or deny his desire to try to get her to open up.

"See you tomorrow," she said, still holding on to her pack.

"It shouldn't take me long," he said. "I'll be back before noon."

"Noon," she repeated as though committing it to memory.

"Yes. Well, good night," he said, and damn if he didn't feel a pull toward touching her lips with his and double damn if she didn't seem to broadcast the hope he would do just that.

They both stepped back at the same time. As he walked down the short hallway back to the kitchen, he heard the door close and the lock click behind him.

He'd never been around a woman who sent so many mixed messages. In her unguarded moments, he liked her—she was amusing and interesting and so beautiful it was hard not to stare at her. That hair! Like gold, smooth and long and framing a perfect oval face. But when she got tense, whoa, back off. She'd all but bitten his father's head off. Why?

Was it just nerves at finding herself in what she considered the enemy camp? His dad could be formidable. Maybe that's all it was.

Or maybe it was something else....

AFTER A RESTLESS NIGHT, Kate found that her window looked out over the ranch yard affording a decent view of Frankie leaving the house and crossing to a picture-perfect barn. It was the first time she'd really had a chance to watch him from a distance.

He wasn't nearly as burly as Luke but easily twice as striking. Luke had had a gentle nature to go along with his brute strength. She put him out of her mind, determined to stay strong.

Frankie came out of the barn a little later leading a saddled horse. He walked it over to a horse trailer attached to a big white truck. Once the horse was tucked safely inside, he drove the rig out of the yard. She knew little of how ranches operated, but she had to assume he was driving to a certain point and then riding the rest of the way on horseback.

A pang of desire hit her hard. How desperately did she want to be in that truck with Frankie, free to go looking for a horse and her baby? Who didn't love a baby horse? Free to do ordinary things, free to just be herself. The pang was immediately followed by shame. She spent the next fifteen minutes braiding her shower-damp hair and dressing, then strapped on her backpack and left her room.

A pleasant-looking woman of about fifty turned as Kate walked into the kitchen. Kate had assumed no one else was awake and so she was caught off guard and stumbled to a halting stop. But this was good. She'd been worried about taking a horse without asking and this way she wouldn't have to do that.

"Harry had to leave. Some trouble with the

dang water pump. I'm Grace, Harry's wife. I assume you're Kate?"

"Yes," Kate said, shaking the woman's hand.

"Sorry I wasn't here when you arrived," Grace continued. "My daughter had a few twinges."

"I thought it was Frankie's brother having the baby," she said.

"That's right, but Gerard is married to my daughter." She laughed. "It's a long story. Get Frankie to tell it to you." She poured a mug from the coffeepot and set it on the counter in front of Kate. "I heard you were going to sleep in today. Frankie left a bit ago. I'm afraid you missed him."

"I just couldn't sleep anymore," Kate said, which was the truth. She looked at the cup of coffee, debating whether to be polite and take a sip or admit she didn't drink the stuff. Politeness won, but one taste later, she put down the cup. Her face must have reflected what she'd tasted because Grace winced.

"I brew it strong for this crew. I'll make a new pot—"

"No, that's okay. It's such a lovely morning. Would you mind if I borrowed a horse? I spent my teenage summers working at a dude ranch so I'm comfortable with animals."

"That's a grand idea. There's a red mare out in the barn that Pike's girlfriend, Sierra, adores."

"That sounds great. Thanks."

"You're welcome." She paused for a second before adding, "If you're riding out to the ghost town, you'll need directions or you'll get lost. And listen, dear, don't feel embarrassed about wanting to come here and get a feel for things. I think your concern for your forefathers' reputations is admirable."

"Thank you," Kate said, uncomfortable with the unwarranted praise this kind woman gave so generously. "For now, I'll just stay by the river. That way I can't get lost."

As if she wasn't already…

Chapter Five

Kate strapped her backpack on the back of the saddle and rode down the small lane that ran parallel to the river. The morning sun beating down on her shoulders helped ease some of the tension of the morning.

She wished she'd had the means to buy a cell phone. She'd given Rose the Hastingses' phone number in case of an emergency, but she could imagine all sorts of things going wrong that Rose might not think of as an emergency. Kate wasn't sure if Gram recognized Kate as her granddaughter or not, but it did seem pretty clear that Kate's presence and the home she'd lived in for fifty years were the very foundation of what little stability she still had.

Kate had promised her dying grandfather she would keep that house as long as her grandmother lived. Trouble was, his illness had eaten up every available penny. The Hastingses didn't seem quite as ruthless as they'd been portrayed, but she'd also been assured they hadn't the slightest idea what she was looking for even existed. Since her subterfuge actually hurt no one, why did it feel so bad?

She rode past a smaller house set on the hillside with a view of the river. This must be Grace's daughter's house and just as that thought surfaced, a very pregnant woman about her own age, opened the door and stepped outside carrying a basket and heading for a fenced garden. She was small in stature with light brown hair and a smiling, warm face. She waved. "Are you Kate West?" she called. "Where's Frankie?"

Kate stifled a sigh. How was she supposed to conduct a covert search when everyone was so dang friendly! "Out looking for a mare and her foal. Are you Grace's daughter?"

"Yes. Are you going for a ride by the river?"

Grateful she'd been up-front about her plans, Kate nodded. "It's too nice to stay indoors."

"I know." She cradled her baby bulge and added, "I miss riding. I also miss my waist and my feet and being able to bend over. Well, I won't keep you, have fun."

"Thanks," Kate called and rode off down the road until it ended and only a trail meandered closer to the water. As the horse made her way along the trail, Kate thought about the details she'd been given that would hopefully help her locate what she was after.

Number one: a bend in this river, the Bowline, and somewhere within a mile or two of this exact spot. There was just such a bend right smack in front of the main ranch house but hopefully, there were others. She didn't even want to think about the possibility of conducting a search out in the open like that.

Two: there had once been a small well to supply water to a cabin that had burned down several years before the information was recorded. Three: a snagged tree. Four: a view of an unnamed mountaintop. Five: a rock that had been described as looking like a bonnet.

The trouble was pretty obvious: rivers change course and while maps certainly existed a hundred years before, the kinds of details she'd been given were flexible. Trees rotted, rock foundations disappeared under vegetation, fires swept the landscape, large boulders eroded or were now underwater, mountains visible once were now camouflaged by a forest. The most reliable source of information on all these things was the Hastings family but, of course, she couldn't ask them.

Greg Abernathy had tried to prepare her for what she might find, but being out along uninhabited, overgrown riverfront turned out to be daunting. She glimpsed a small rise ahead and aimed for that, hoping it would provide an overview of the area. Once she'd reached that higher elevation, she looked in all directions, then got off the mare and walked to the edge of the small bluff. A bend in the river lay directly beneath her position. There was even a rock although it didn't look much like a bonnet from this vantage point, but she was hopeful. If this was the spot, she could leave the next day after pretending to rethink her stand on the documentary.

She took the horse's reins in her hand and began the search for the way down to the riverbank below. The sun had already risen high in the sky and it was hot in with the overgrown berry vines and weeds. It didn't take long until perspiration dotted her forehead. The vines were young and vigorous, their thorns like little sabers tearing at her clothes. Behind her, the horse skittered along on the uneven ground. It took about twenty minutes before they stepped onto a narrow rocky shore. She untied the backpack, set it on the ground and opened it. Behind her, the forest crowded the shoreline.

Time to get to work.

FRANKIE KNEW THERE were some days on a ranch—or anywhere else—that nothing seemed to go right. A simple job could take three times as long as expected when equipment broke or helpers didn't show up on time. But nothing slapped a wild card down on the table like dealing with animals.

Today was not one of those days. He arrived out at the Bywater pasture, unloaded the previously saddled gelding, tightened the cinch and rode thirty minutes down the gully toward Ten Cent Creek. He ran into the bay mare and her foal standing apart from the rest of the ranch horses who spent their off time in this pasture. The colt was a long-legged, spindly-looking little guy with white socks and a blaze down his nose. While the mare was dusty and had stickers caught in her mane and tail, the newborn practically sparkled. Frankie dismounted and checked them out—both appeared well. He fed the mare an apple he'd stuffed in his saddlebag, slid a halter around her head and mounted his own horse. Leading the mare, the colt frolicking behind her, they made their way uphill to the transport. He loaded all three animals and got back in the truck.

The whole thing had taken just a little over two hours, and by the time he drove back into the yard, it was well before noon. There would be plenty of time to take Kate out to the ghost town and show her the hanging tree although he needed to come up with a more sensitive name for the thing first.

He tied his mount to the railing of the fence as he released the mare and colt into a stall inside the barn. He made sure they had fresh feed and water, then crossed the yard to the house. Grace sat at the table hand-sewing the hem of a yellow sleeper. Kinsey and Gerard had elected not to know the sex of their first child, preferring the old-fashioned wait-and-see approach. Grace, who treated Lily's son like her grandson, was excited about having a baby around the house.

She looked up as he entered. "You're back early," she said.

"Things just fell into place," he explained. He looked down the hall. "Where is everybody?"

"Today is Lily's turn to help at Charlie's school. Your dad spent part of the morning fooling with that antique water pump, then he went to sign some papers at the bank. Your brothers are out with a couple of summer hires windrowing the hay in the south fields."

"What about Kate? Is she still asleep?"

"Heavens no. She left soon after you did."

He'd been headed toward the refrigerator to grab a bottle of juice but stopped short. "She didn't sleep in?"

"No."

"Did she ride out to the ghost town?"

"She said she was going to stay close to the river. I saw her riding toward Kinsey's house."

"The river? Did she say why?"

"Not really. She didn't say a whole lot."

"Did she ask you any awkward questions?"

"Awkward?"

"She's trying to get a feel for us and find out about the film, so she's bound to want to know about things."

"I can't say she asked anything except to borrow a horse. Truthfully, she seemed a little preoccupied. But finding Mr. Dalton yesterday—maybe that upset her. It would have gotten to me."

"Yeah," he said. He turned toward the door. "I think I'll see if I can intercept her."

"Good luck," Grace said. "Oh, and tell her someone named Rose called. She didn't want to leave a message except to ask that Kate call her back."

"I'll tell her if I find her." He left the kitchen without the juice and got back on his horse, directing it down the road toward Gerard's house. By now he was used to the nagging feeling that he was playing catch-up with Kate. He had to figure her out. Something was weird.

She had limited time, or so she claimed, so why was she out sightseeing? The passionate, determined woman in the Seattle restaurant had

had one goal—stop the documentary. Now she was here, now she could investigate what it was she so opposed but instead…something didn't add up.

"Stop being so suspicious," he told himself as he passed his brother's house and kept going. There were fresh tracks leading beside the river. Curious, he followed. They disappeared up the rocky slope of a small knoll that he rode to the top. He'd been up and down this river many times over the course of his life and he knew from there he could see several hundred feet of both sides of the river before another bend hid it from view. He got off the horse and stood there with wildflowers brushing against his legs until a sound drew him toward the edge.

He saw Ginger tied to a tree on the beach below. Kate's big bulky backpack sat on the rocks near the horse but there was no sign of Kate. Thinking he would climb down to make sure everything was okay, he began to turn but movement off in the forest caught his eye and he stopped. Not sure why he did so, he stepped back a little and watched as Kate emerged from the shadows under the trees.

She walked out into the sunshine, holding what appeared to be a short machete in her hand.

A machete? Where had that come from? What in the world was she doing?

Her hair had come loose from her braid and sported all sorts of leaves and debris while her windbreaker had a three-inch gash down one arm. She folded the machete into a towel and put it in her pack and then she raised her arms to pull off her jacket. This time, both the light windbreaker and the T-shirt beneath it slid over her head.

He told himself to look away but he didn't budge. For one thing, he didn't want movement from him to make her look up and catch him watching her. For another, he couldn't bear not to look.

She dumped her clothes on the top of the pack and walked to the water's edge, her gold hair trailing down her mostly bare back catching every ray of sunshine, her surprisingly lush bosom bouncing gently as she moved. She knelt at the water's edge, cupped her hands and splashed water up onto her face and chest, washing drops of blood off her arms and pushing back her hair from her face before standing and staring back into the forest.

Half-naked, damp splotches on her sky blue bra, skin glistening with water, she was nothing short of breathtaking. He knew she would never forgive him if she caught him watching her and willed her to turn away so he could get out of there. It had been a stroke of luck that he was upwind from Ginger so she hadn't caught scent of his horse and given him away. How long could he depend on luck?

Finally, Kate leaned over, separated her T-shirt from her jacket and pulled it over her head. Any second now and she would remount Ginger and retreat up this hill—it was the quickest way to the ranch. He waited until her back was to him and, hoping the water breaking over the rocks in the river a few feet away from her would disguise any noise he made from above, led the horse to the other side of the knoll, mounted and rode downhill. He kept going until he was almost back on the road to Gerard's place, and then he turned around and started back the direction he'd just come.

With any luck, it would appear he'd only now ridden out to find her and she would never know he'd seen her on the beach.

The unintentional display of partial nudity aside, however, the basic question still existed. What had she been doing in the forest with a machete?

KATE FOUGHT THE urge to continue her search. She knew she couldn't get discouraged after one failure but the thought had begun to cross her mind that it was unlikely this venture would be completed within one day.

It was closing in on noon as she left the rise, and as soon as she headed back, thoughts of her grandmother flooded her head. After over a year of being responsible for the woman's care every second of every day, being away felt wrong. She knew total control was an illusion, but it was her current life's main motivator— if she was present, she could fix things, anticipate trouble, keep all the little plates spinning on their poles.

The red mare whinnied and Kate's mind focused back on the here and now. She glanced ahead to find Frankie riding toward her. She smoothed her hair off her forehead and tugged her T-shirt away from her damp skin.

"Hi," he called as they met on the path. The horses sniffed each other as Frankie looked directly into her eyes. "Have a nice ride?"

"Very nice," she said.

"Where'd you go?"

"I found a rock close to the water and read for a while," she said, biting her lip and hoping he didn't ask what she was reading because her mind was a sudden and complete blank.

"Did you do anything else?"

"Like what?" she said, suddenly nervous.

"Oh, I don't know. Take a walk, maybe? There's a lot of pretty forest around the river."

"It looks pretty dense," she said.

"Hmm. By the way, you got a call from some-one named Rose."

"Rose called! What—"

"Grace said she didn't leave a message except for you to call her back." He dug in his pocket and extracted his cell phone, which he handed to her. "I'm going to ride ahead and make sand-wiches. Take your time."

As she accepted his phone, their fingers brushed and the next thing she knew, he'd gripped her wrist and gently turned her arm. He was staring at the scratch she'd acquired in the woods that was once again bloody. "What happened?" he asked.

"I…tripped into some blackberry vines. I can be such a klutz."

He stared at her an additional few seconds, then gently dropped her hand. "See you in a while," he said, kicked his horse and rode away, his figure tall and straight in his saddle. He left her with the distinct feeling that he suspected something. There was no way, though, none at all. She turned around to make sure her back-pack wasn't hanging open revealing a bunch of tools, but it was buckled tight.

Unable to fight the urge to check on Gram another moment, she pulled the mare to the side of the path and punched in Rose's cell number.

"Is something wrong?" Kate asked the minute Rose responded.

"It's been quite a night," Rose said.

"Is Gram—"

"She's just fine, honey. I don't even think her toes got wet."

"What? What happened?"

"The hot water heater broke," Rose said. "I had to call the plumber in the middle of the night because I didn't know how to fix it. He said it's been leaking through a corroded pipe for a long time. It's in that closet near the utility room and it managed to do some significant damage. Anyway, the plumber advised us to get out of the house until it can be dried out and checked for mold spores on account of how long it's been leaking. I'm afraid you lost the carpet…anyway, we're okay and your grandmother has already forgotten anything happened."

"Where is she?"

"I wanted to bring her to my house but I have three cats, two big dogs and a grandson living in my basement. I finally checked her into a care facility for dementia patients. They had an empty room and agreed to a weeklong stay upon her doctor's recommendation. He gave it and I settled her in there this morning."

The very thing Kate had been killing herself to prevent had happened the minute she left Seattle. Her grandmother was in a home. "I don't know what to do," she heard herself say.

"There's nothing you can do," Rose said. "Your grandmother is safe. Mr. Abernathy contacted your insurance company. You're covered for a lot of what needs to be done. There will be a deductible, of course, and they ask that you call to give authorization. I'll visit your grandmother every day."

"Is she terribly upset? Maybe I should come home."

"Suit yourself," Rose said. "But the truth is she almost looked happy to see other people. Of course she's asking them all if they know where Dennis is, but there are a lot more people to ask now." She paused a moment before adding, "I'm sorry to say this, but she'll forget you're in Seattle two minutes after you've left her side whether it's now or a week from now."

In her heart, Kate was already on a plane landing in Seattle. She could picture walking into Gram's room. But the smile of relief and welcome she tried to visualize on Gram's face just wouldn't come. Those expressions and the reasoning to create them had disappeared a while back.

"You're right," she said at last. "I have to see this through. Where exactly is she?"

"Pine Hill. Here's their number and the one for the insurance people."

Kate dug a pen out of the backpack and wrote the numbers on her arm. Then she clicked off the phone and immediately dialed the facility. She talked to the manager of the home and was assured Gram was wandering the circular hallways and had eaten lunch with the others.

She hung up from that call still riddled with indecision, torn between staying and leaving, angry at herself for going away in the first place. She put her hands over her face as guilt and remorse flooded through her body, gripping handfuls of Ginger's russet mane to keep from sliding off the saddle.

Where was the woman who had held back tears? Who was this blubbering waterworks of a human being? She sat up, mopped her face and squared her shoulders. Enough was enough.

Chapter Six

Kate was relieved when Kinsey didn't appear at her door. She knew she must look puffy and tear-streaked. In a perfect world, she could beam herself back to the bedroom without having to talk to anyone.

But that was not to be, for as she slid from the saddle and took the mare's reins to enter the barn, a good-looking guy with sun-browned skin exited. She tried averting her face, but there was no polite way to do that.

"Are you okay?" he said at once.

"Yes." Knowing her face told a different story, she added, "Darn allergies."

"I'm Pike," he added, offering a smile that evoked thoughts of Frankie. "You have to be Kate West. Welcome to Hastings Ridge."

"Thanks."

"Let me take care of Ginger for you."

"She's a sweetheart," Kate said, patting the horse's sleek shoulder.

"That she is. Sierra adores her."

"She's your girlfriend, right?"

"Yes, she's my girl. Well, her and Daisy, my dog. You might not mention that to anyone else, though."

"I won't say a word," she said, marveling at how comfortable this guy was in his skin. He looked a little like Frankie, but there was something more peaceful about him. He began unstrapping Kate's backpack from the saddle. She couldn't exactly demand he not touch it so she waited for the inevitable comment about its clumsy weight. The contents clanked and Pike's eyebrows furrowed, but he made no comment as he handed the pack to Kate and took the reins from her.

Kate thanked him and walked toward the house, the backpack an unwieldy burden thumping against her legs. Sure enough, a van with Washington state plates and the company's name, LOGO, had pulled in next to Frankie's car. She walked into the kitchen to find Frankie signing what appeared to be a stack of business papers while Gary Dodge, a lanky man of about fifty with graying sandy hair and wire-framed glasses, stood nearby. He looked at Kate and reached out for the backpack. "Let me relieve you of that—"

"No, that's okay," she said, hugging it against her chest.

"It's good to see you again," Gary said. "Frankie was just telling me about Dave Dalton. Man, that's terrible."

"Yes," she said.

"Have you heard anything more from the police?"

This last question was directed at Frankie who shook his head though his gaze was glued to Kate's face. "Not a word. Don't really expect to unless there's a problem of some kind."

Gary nodded and looked back at Kate. "Well, what do you think of this beautiful ranch and the fine family that owns it?"

"Everything is…amazing," Kate said.

"Nice and subtle, Gary," Frankie said.

Gary grinned. "Just want to make sure things are okay. Before Grace walked over to Kinsey and Gerard's house she mentioned you'd gone riding. I gather you already investigated the river this morning."

"Investigated?" Kate said, struggling to keep the alarm out of her voice. She glanced at Frankie who was watching her closely. "I don't know about that, exactly," she said. "It's very peaceful by the water and Frankie had ranch business so I had a little free time."

"Excellent."

"We're about to visit the ghost town," Frankie told Gary. "You're welcome to come along."

"I have to get back to Seattle for a meeting this evening. I just wanted you to sign this contract and I also wanted to tell you some fabulous news."

"We could use good news," Frankie said.

Gary fairly beamed. "I heard from Pat Lowell. He's spoken to the other man he had lined up. Turns out he isn't a descendant himself but his wife was directly related to a guy who claimed to know all about the robbery."

"What man?"

"Dare we hope the missing man?" Gary said with drama. "The fourth robber, the one who got away. If so, it looks like he was a drifter from out of town. This guy Pat talked to, his name is Jerry Stillwater, inherited his deceased wife's mother's estate when she died. He found a bundle of old letters that had been in their family for decades. Pat is pretty sure he'll eventually be able to pinpoint the exact location of the missing gold that was stolen from the bank. According to the letters, the gold never left this area. If he can do that and the gold is still buried here and we can find it, can you imagine what a great ending it would make for the documentary?"

"I can't believe this," Frankie said with an unmistakable edge of excitement to his voice. "Have you seen these letters yourself?"

"Not yet. I just got his call this morning. Pat's engaging an expert down in Boise to go over them—apparently there's fairly significant water damage to contend with. He says he saw nothing that mentioned the Bowline River but he did pick out Ten Cent Creek and the hills near the area called Bywater. There's also some mention of a cave. He's afraid to keep looking until the papers are stabilized but his expert says it should be done within a few days."

"Is he sure about the Bowline? It's the biggest river around here. I always thought that if the gold was still around, that's where it would be." He suddenly narrowed his eyes and glanced quickly at Kate and away again. She swallowed hard. A guilty conscience was a heavy, ponderous burden she wasn't used to managing and fancied every stray uncomfortable thought that popped into her head appeared on her face.

But what could he know? Nothing. She was being paranoid. "Who would the gold belong to?" she asked to diffuse the speculation in his eyes.

"The lawyers can figure that out later," Frankie said.

"Won't your father insist it's his?" Kate said. Everything Greg Abernathy had told her about the man suggested he would never let anything valuable leave his land no matter to whom it belonged.

Frankie cast her an annoyed frown but said nothing. She shouldn't have said anything.

"Ownership isn't the issue right now," Gary said. "The discovery is what's important—well, that and the identity of that elusive fourth man. This could be the wow moment we've been missing."

Frankie apparently allowed his suspicions to subside as he broke into a wondrous, wistful smile. "Wouldn't that be something," he said softly. He glanced down at Kate yet again. "Maybe there will be something in those letters that will exonerate your great-great-great-grandfather and his brother."

"Or possibly reveal the extent of their involvement," Gary warned.

Kate nodded. Frankie's concern for her sensibilities despite his obvious misgivings touched her more than she could bear to admit and she wasn't positive how to respond. She'd always thought getting invited to the ranch would be the hard part of this situation—well, that and uncovering the treasure; she hadn't figured on the difficulty of maintaining her point of view in light of the fact that when it came to the documentary, she didn't have one. But what she did have were gigantic concerns for her grandmother's safety and that's what mattered, that's what she had to keep in mind at all times.

However, the historian they kept talking about puzzled her. Why hadn't this Pat Lowell researched her phony claims? Maybe he was too deeply involved in these letters to even think of it but it seemed odd.

"I'm not afraid of the truth," she said and wondered if anyone had ever told a bigger lie.

"Neither are we," Frankie said.

FRANKIE HELD HIS tongue as they approached the trail paralleling the stream that led from the back of the house up the hill and eventually to the plateau above. But thoughts and images churned in his head until he finally had to say something. "Tell me one thing," he said as they crossed the stream single file. "Are you really here because of your relatives or is there another reason?"

"Another reason?" she said, and her voice sounded so surprised he shot a look over his shoulder to glimpse her face. "Like what?"

"Just what I said. Are you here because of

Earl and Samuel Bates, or is there something else you're not telling me?"

"Of course there are things I'm not telling you."

"That is a nonanswer," he protested and cast her another glance.

"I can assure you, however, that I would not be a guest of your family and work against you."

"Well, pardon me for saying so, but you seem to have a lot on your...mind."

She didn't respond as they ducked their heads to pass under some low-hanging branches. He stopped talking. Holding a conversation in that manner was pointless. So much of what Kate said showed on her face. Without being able to see her, he felt lost.

The path hadn't been used a lot since spring and for once wasn't muddy. It was a pleasant ride in the shade of the trees, but he waited until they erupted out of the heavy canopy of trees onto the plateau to restart their discussion. The ghost town was off a couple of miles to the right. He directed them left, toward the scattered oaks that dotted the rugged landscape.

"I have another question," he said as he reined in his horse to keep pace with hers.

She glanced at him. "Go ahead," she said.

He measured his words carefully. "Why are you so negative about my father?"

She looked away from his face but answered immediately. "He kind of reminds me of my own father, kind of full of himself. I shouldn't have judged him so quickly, though. I apologize."

He smiled as he shook his head. "That's not going to wash, Kate," he said. He corrected the course to avoid a gully and dug in his saddlebag for the sandwiches he'd tucked there. He handed one to her. "See, I remember you said something snarly about him the first time we met," he added as he unwrapped roast beef and cheddar on sourdough. "If you'd never met him, then why—"

"Someone told me he was…selfish," she said, her cheeks turning a delicate pink as she stared at the unwrapped sandwich in her hand.

"Who told you that?"

"I'd rather not say. Can we drop this? There's no excuse for my behavior, at least none I can offer. I'm sorry."

"Consider the subject dropped."

They rode in silence for a few more minutes, concentrating on the boulders and gullies, the big oak growing ever closer. Frankie ate his sandwich with relish—he could make a mean sandwich if he did say so himself—but he noticed Kate tuck hers away in that giant backpack that never left her side. Did the woman ever eat? At least she was awake, that was something, right?

"This is the tree," Frankie finally said when they rode into the shade underneath the long, sweeping branches. Roots like petrified snakes erupted from the earth and spread outward. "It was smaller back then but big enough for the posse's needs."

"Three people died here," she said softly as she slid out of the saddle. Her hair was back in the long braid and he watched her stare through the limbs above for a moment or two as though getting a feeling for the tragedy the tree had helped commit. He shook his head to dispel a sudden memory of her bare, translucent skin and got off his horse, dropping the lead, knowing it wouldn't wander far away from the shade where a few blades of tender grass undoubtedly looked tasty.

He perched on a root that had reached near chair height. She looked down at him. "Why does your family call you Frankie instead of Frank?"

"Isn't that kind of personal?" he said. As a surprise question from out of the blue, she'd just won the gold medal.

She smiled. "Yes. Sorry."

"To answer your question, my mother is a little bit of a nomad. She's been traveling her whole life and seems totally incapable of stopping. The best thing she ever did for me was to give me a man for a father with three other sons and firm roots. Even then, it was rough growing up with her floating in and out of my life like a butterfly."

"Is she still alive?"

"Oh, yes. I don't hear from her often, but every once in a while, she shows up with a few fascinating stories and a breezy kiss and then she's off again."

"Did she grow up around here?"

"I'm not sure where she grew up. Dad says the first he was aware of her was when she appeared at the ranch one day lost. She said she was looking for someone but he can't remember who it was. He'd just had his fourth divorce, she was a real beauty, and one thing followed another. They were married soon after and then I was born."

Most people commented on the number of marriages his father had willingly entered. In fact, Grace was wife number seven, or lucky number seven as Harry Hastings affectionately called her. But this information didn't seem to lodge for a second in Kate's mind. "I wonder who your mother was looking for."

He shrugged. "Dad says she never mentioned anything about it again."

"Can't you just ask her?"

He smiled. "No one can answer a question and say as little as my mother," he said. "Except for you," he added under his breath as he met her blue-eyed gaze. "The past doesn't interest her much. Maybe she just wanted to meet my dad and used that as an excuse."

"And all this ties into your name because?"

"Oh, yeah. Because she named me in honor of her grandmother's father. In a way, my name is a small link to my shrouded maternal past."

"It seems kind of strange, doesn't it?"

"In a way, I suppose it is. Dad theorizes that Mom was wounded as a child in a way she couldn't bear to face and that she reinvented herself and resolved to move forward and not look back. He thinks I'm the only living relative she has. She didn't even tell me that tidbit about my name until I was eighteen and in a spot of… trouble. Okay, this is way more story than you bargained for." He stood up and gazed down at her. "Now it's your turn."

"What do you mean?"

He took a deep breath and hoped his unplanned object lesson in sharing had made an impression. "Forgive me for bringing this up. Your grandmother has Alzheimer's, doesn't she? And Dennis, who is he?"

For a second, he thought she wouldn't answer,

but then an almost imperceptible sigh escaped her lips. "Dennis was my grandfather. He died a little over a year ago. Gram had been getting bad before that but with him gone, she really went downhill."

"And you moved in to save her."

"Yes." Her eyes suddenly flooded and she bit her lip. He wondered how to comfort her without incurring her wrath, but when she covered her face with her hands and her shoulders shook, he threw caution to the wind and just put his arms around her.

As she leaned against him and allowed herself to cry unabashedly, the strangest sensation stole over him. Had he held her before? Not really, but this didn't feel like the first time their bodies had touched. In fact it felt like he'd held her in his arms a thousand times before and that it was destiny he hold her a thousand times again.

Okay, this was stupid. He told himself to release her, to step back, not to touch her. None of those things happened. It was as though he was frozen into place and he was suddenly afraid of breaking this connection with her, afraid it would hurt one or both of them and that made no sense at all.

He looked down at the top of her head and somehow his face drifted toward her and he felt his lips touch her hair. She immediately startled and looked up at him, her moist blue eyes deep and secretive.

Her delicate pink lips all but called his name. Who was he to resist the siren call of destiny?

Chapter Seven

The kiss was almost over before it started, but for the instant it existed, Frankie's imagination seemed to shoot through the stars. Then Kate pulled away from him and stood staring into his eyes.

He swallowed a knot of alarm. He'd kissed any number of women in his lifetime and most with a far deeper sense of intimacy, but this was different, just as holding her was different. "Kate, I am...sorry, I...so sorry," he blubbered, unsure what to say, longing to reach for her again but shoving his hands in his pockets instead. What in the world had come over him?

"It's my fault," she said quickly, her voice trembling.

"How could it be your fault? No, I take full responsibility. My gosh, you're a guest here—"

"I know it's hard to believe, but I used to be

the most self-confident woman you'd ever want to meet. I never, ever cried."

"That's not hard to believe," he said gently.

"I hardly remember that girl. Now, all I do is second-guess my decisions and regret…poor Luke—"

She stopped abruptly as though shocked she'd said too much and blinked back tears as she looked up into the boughs overhead.

Who the heck was Luke? "It's this tree," he offered. "Gerard says the aura of the tragedy that happened here still lingers. I don't know, maybe he's right."

"What do you mean?" she asked, sniffing back the last of her tears and wiping at her eyes.

For a second he debated telling her anything else that would upset her. But he didn't have long to convince her the documentary would be honest and truthful so he waded in feet first. "Do you know the history of what happened after the hangings?"

She shook her head.

"They left the bodies here to rot, both out of fury and to serve as a warning to the man who got away. Can you imagine how awful that must have been for every living creature around here? We knew this story as kids. It was exactly the ghoulish kind of information little boys love. When Gerard was pretty young, a group of older kids tied him to this tree. Dad didn't find him until way after dark and Gerard has never really gotten over it."

"That's terrible," she said, shuddering.

"It was. And what happened a hundred years ago was a million times worse, and I am extremely sorry that your family was involved. And yet, that's what happened. That's what history is, just the past, nothing more. It's what we do with it that matters. And as compelling as the tree's story became, I have to admit it's the town that's always fascinated me. I know you need to leave the ranch very soon, but I'd like you to see the town before you go, I'd like you to imagine it alive and teeming with people and hope."

He could see the wheels turning in her head though he didn't know why they would.

"As a matter of fact, I have a little extra time," she said carefully. "My hot water heater exploded or leaked or something. The house has to be empty for a week. Gram is in a…home."

"I'm sorry," he said. His instinct was to reach out and touch her arm or squeeze her hand, but no way was he touching her again. "Don't you need to return to Seattle?"

"I can't leave here yet," she mumbled. "I need to see this through first."

"See what through? Whether or not you oppose the making of a documentary? This isn't more important than your grandmother."

"It's dreadfully important to me…and her," Kate insisted.

He shook his head. "How can you be concerned about the reputations of two men you never met while the grandmother you love and support—"

"Don't tell me how to support my grandmother," she interrupted, her eyes suddenly flashing.

"I wasn't," he said, but he knew she was right, that's exactly what he'd done.

"You don't know my whole story," she added. "You don't know about Grandpa or the bills or what the last year has been like."

His eyebrows tilted. "There's a reason for that," he said. "You haven't told me."

She shook her head. "Please, can't you just mind your own business?"

"Sure I can. Wait, this ranch is my business. This documentary is my business."

"Why are you so obsessed with making this film?"

He started to explain but caught himself short. "Oh, no you don't. You're switching the attention away from yourself."

She rubbed her forehead as though it hurt. His head hurt, too. How had they gotten to this point? Was he crazy? His whole reason for having her here was to convince her to see things his way. *Not* to kiss her. *Not* to follow her around. *Not* to alienate her.

They couldn't go forward until the air was clear and his gut told him it had to start with her explaining what she'd been doing with that machete and why she'd lied about her morning activities. Was there some way she knew about the gold? How was that possible when Gary had only heard that morning? But why else was she clearing brush in the forest?

But he knew she wouldn't explain herself if he asked, she'd just get sneakier. And, too, there were those few minutes of not so gallant voyeurism he'd have to explain away and he really didn't want to go there, especially now. "This is getting us nowhere," he finally grumbled.

"I know."

"Just be honest with me. Am I spinning my wheels when you've already plotted a media blitz?"

"No," she said, for once meeting his gaze straight on. He heard no equivocation in her voice. "I'm taking this more seriously than you'll ever know."

"You understand this makes no sense."

"Not to you. It does to me."

"One more thing. I will not stand by and

watch my family hurt in any way. I owe them more than you'll ever know and no one gets past me to threaten them."

"Are you accusing me of wanting to hurt your family?"

"Not entirely. But damn, something is going on with you. Right?"

"No," she said firmly.

Could he trust her? Hell, no. "It's getting late," he finally grumbled. "Let's ride out to the ghost town."

"I'd like to do it tomorrow," she said.

"What?"

"Unless you have previous plans—"

"I have no plans," he said, but even he heard the sarcasm running through his voice. "Summer on a ranch is just one big vacation," he added. He shook his head and kicked at a root. "Sorry. Okay, we'll do it your way. Tomorrow morning—"

"How about the afternoon instead?"

His eyes narrowed. "Would you rather one of my brothers take you?"

"No."

"You're sure?"

"Would you rather one of them—"

"No," he admitted. "No."

"We can behave ourselves, right?" she added. He shook his head as a reluctant smile twitched his lips. "Yeah, I guess we can," he said but all he could think of was this guy Luke. Who was he?

As THEY LEFT the cover of the path by the stream and emerged into the main yard of the ranch house, Kate decided not to tell Frankie her real plans to go to the river. It was obvious he knew something about her didn't ring true and that heartfelt speech he'd made about protecting his family hadn't fallen on deaf ears.

If he felt she represented a threat, she'd be gone in a New York second.

"I've got some work to do before dinner," Frankie announced as they led the horses into the barn.

"I guess I'll go take a nap," she said doing her best to take the pack off the horse without struggling with its weight.

"Wait just a second," he said.

She waited as he stared at her, his mind obviously racing. He finally sighed and hitched his hands on his waist. "I pride myself on a couple of things," he said. "One of them is my ability to read people. But you fly off my radar. I'm constantly trying to figure you out. I know I messed things up this afternoon. In some ways it's really clear how I got off track but in other ways… I don't know."

How did she respond to this? He was absolutely right about her. A wave of shame washed through her stomach making her glad she hadn't eaten.

"I feel like all we do is apologize to each other," he added.

"I know," she said at last. "Listen. Tomorrow afternoon you're going to show me the ghost town and I promise to do my best to see it through your eyes. I'm going to think about what you've said about history. Maybe I overreacted about all this. At any rate, the day after tomorrow, I'll be gone and your life will go back to normal."

"You'll be gone," he repeated but his voice didn't sound as happy about that prospect as she assumed it would. "I know you don't eat a lot, but Grace plans dinner for around seven."

"I'm looking forward to it. I want to get to know your family."

His expression clearly said he was once again confused by her comment and she couldn't blame him. She fought the urge to just tell him the truth.

A few minutes later, he drove the big truck out of the yard and across the bridge. She watched it climb the road on the other side of the river until it disappeared, then she saddled a fresh horse, tied the backpack to the saddle and took off down the road toward Kinsey's house and the river beyond.

Kinsey was outside again, and if anything, she looked bigger than she had that morning. As she was cutting roses near the road, Kate slowed the horse and stopped to say hello.

"Do you know what you're having?" Kate asked.

Kinsey shook her head. "Gerard didn't want to know. I kind of hope it's a girl because of Heidi."

"Heidi?"

"Oh, I'm sorry. Heidi was Gerard's daughter with his first wife, Ann. Both of them died in an accident before Gerard and I met. I don't know, maybe it would be better to have a boy. I guess it's all academic anyway, I mean, the baby will be whatever the baby will be."

"It's very exciting," Kate said.

"I think so, too. Babies are great, aren't they?"

Kate nodded. She hadn't really thought much about babies in her life but there was no way she was going to rain on the maternal joy glowing in Kinsey's eyes. "You bet. I can hardly wait." Wanting to change the subject, she added, "I haven't met your husband yet, but everyone seems to love him."

"They have to, they're all related to him,"

Kinsey said with a smile. She took a sudden deep breath and put a hand on her belly.

"Are you okay?" Kate asked, immediately sliding from the saddle and reaching out a hand. The second her feet hit the ground, her head began to spin and she stumbled. Kinsey was the one who did the steadying and they both chuckled.

"Lot of help I am," Kate said.

"You all right?"

"I haven't been eating a whole lot for the last couple of months," she explained. "My stomach…well, nerves, you know how it is."

"Come inside and let me make you something."

"Thank you, but I have a sandwich that Frankie gave me. I'll eat that. But what about you? Are you okay?"

"I've been having these contractions all day," Kinsey said. "I guess they're a warm-up for the big event. Gerard came home for lunch a while ago and I had to force him to go mow hay. Between him and my mother sharing the duties of a 24/7 baby watch, I'm going a little nuts."

"Grace said something this morning about how you're her daughter and Gerard is her stepson?"

"That's right. She's actually the reason we met. She asked Gerard to do a favor for her, he was injured while doing it, I helped him find his way home. And that's how I met Grace, Harry's new wife and the mother I never knew I had." Kinsey's eyes filled with tears and she flicked them away with her finger. "I cry at the drop of a hat."

"So do I lately," Kate admitted. "Between crying and sleeping, that's how I spend most of my free time. Frankly, it sucks."

"But it's worth it," Kinsey said.

Kate wasn't sure what she meant unless she was alluding to caring for her grandmother. Of course she was. Everyone here knew everything about everyone else. Coming from a small family, this kind of networking seemed daunting.

"Are you off on another ride?"

"I'm going to read by the river," Kate said. "I guess I better get going."

"Have a nice time," Kinsey said and waved as Kate rode off.

These people were too nice. It made all the deception worse and Kate felt her eyes sting.

"Oh stop sniveling for heaven's sake," she lectured herself and took a deep breath. Maybe this time would be the charm—she sure hoped so.

Chapter Eight

Frankie backed his truck against a cluster of poplar trees that grew on the south side of the river, aiming to conceal it as best he could. He took the binoculars out of their case and left the cab, positioning himself where he had a clear view of the north shore, the side of the river Kate had been exploring this morning. It was the easiest way he could figure out how to see what she was up to without alerting her.

This was another place where the Bowline made a turn, much like the one he'd found her near earlier that day. Here, too, a big boulder stood close to the water's edge. He eventually picked out a trail of whacked vegetation leading back into the trees. Adjusting the glasses, he found she'd cleared a sizeable rock. Snowball, their white gelding, was tied to a nearby branch.

He turned the glasses toward the sparse woods and glimpsed Kate tangled in underbrush. It looked as though she was trying to free herself by attacking the stems low to the ground with the machete.

She finally yanked her leg free and took a deep breath. From this angle, he could see she'd created a kind of makeshift sling and wore it over her shoulder. There, resting against her back, hung a small folding shovel. The weight and clunking sounds coming from her backpack began to make sense.

The plot thickened.

She moved off to the right and untied the horse, then leading him along the shore, disappeared around the bend. Another truck pulled up as Frankie walked back to his own.

"Car trouble?" Gerard asked through the open window.

Frankie leaned against the truck. "Nope, just bird-watching. How's Kinsey doing?"

"Still holding on." He glanced across the river and back at Frankie. "I believe your bird is leading Snowball down the beach," he said with a grin.

Frankie resisted the urge to throw himself to the ground as he turned his head to see Kate retracing her route. He could tell she hadn't seen them. Gerard picked up on his unease and both men stayed silent and still until Kate walked around another bend.

"What's going on with you?" Gerard asked.

"She's up to something."

"What?"

"I don't know. Have you heard about Pat Lowell's belief that he's on the threshold of figuring out if the stolen gold might be still buried around these parts?"

"Yeah. Word gets around. Pete Richards was helping us mow. You remember Pete?"

"Sure. He used to work summers."

"Yeah. He's helping with the mowing. You should have seen his eyes light up when Dad told us what Gary said. There's something about buried treasure, isn't there?"

"Yeah, there is." Frankie paused for a second, then went ahead and added, "Kate's searching for something."

"Are you suggesting she has advance word of the gold and thinks she knows where it is?"

"I don't know what I'm suggesting. I asked Pat to double-check her claim to be related to Earl and Samuel Bates. I'm getting some really weird vibes from her."

"From what I just saw, the girl is a knockout. You sure those vibes aren't sexual?"

"Pretty sure."

"Talk to her."

"I don't know. She's slippery. Pretty, sexy, sweet but slippery. If you ask me it's a guilty conscience. I know something about that. I recognize the symptoms."

"Frankie, take some advice from your oldest brother," Gerard said. "Just tell her exactly what you've seen and heard that alarms you." He glanced at his watch. "I need to get home to stare at Kinsey. She loves it when I do that."

This last line was delivered with a smile and a slap on Frankie's shoulder. As he drove away, Frankie's phone rang and he took it from his pocket. Pat Lowell's name glowed on the screen. Good.

IT WAS A smaller than average group that gathered around the table for dinner. Grace talked about her pending grandchild, Harry talked about rebuilding a mile of fence over by the Bywater pasture, Kate asked seemingly disjointed questions about the changes in the Bowline River and Frankie surreptitiously watched Kate.

Why was she asking about the river? Pat Lowell's call should have been reassuring. He'd assured Frankie she was exactly who she said she was. Frankie had asked Pat if it was possible she knew something about the missing gold. Pat had laughed. "Absolutely not. That girl hasn't done anything but try to keep her grandmother from having to enter a state-run home for the past thirteen months. Before that she taught kids. I can see where her hacking around the forest seems odd, but if she's not hurting anything, I'd give her a break. She minored in science, maybe she's just curious. At any rate, I didn't find anything negative."

Frankie's thoughts returned to those around him when he caught his father's next comment. "Oh, the Bowline has changed course a lot even in my lifetime," he said, apparently in response to one of Kate's questions. "But before that, there was the flood of 1926. That washed out the riverfront part of Green Ridge—that's what the ghost town was called back in its day—and the old bridge. By then, the town was all but abandoned because of the robbery. The river itself shifted course. Rocks that had been submerged were suddenly on the beach. You know how it is. There was also a fire that took out a couple of houses, but that was before the town was even established."

Grace's phone rang halfway through the meal, and she answered it at once and listened intently before hanging up. "Kinsey and Gerard are on their way to the urgent care facility," she reported with a smile. "Oh, Frankie. I spoke to your mother today."

"Mom?" Frankie said, surprised. "Where did

you see her? I didn't even know she was back in Idaho."

"I didn't see her and she's not back though she will be tomorrow evening. She lost your phone number so she called Harry and he was in the shower so I answered. She was in a rush but said you can expect her tomorrow night for a couple of hours. She wants to talk to you."

"Sure," Frankie said, meeting Kate's gaze. Man, when it rained, it poured. He wasn't sure he was up to handling the fickleness of his mother on top of the perplexity of Kate.

Grace insisted on cleaning up the table, saying she was too nervous to sit. Harry grumbled about driving down to see if the pump was working yet. Frankie asked Kate to take a walk with him.

She tried to squirm out of it but he persisted. "I'll wait for you out on the bench by the back door." He said it with enough finality that he could see her bristle. "Take a damn walk with me, will you, please?"

THERE WAS JUST about nothing on earth Kate wanted to do less than be alone with Frankie Hastings.

Well, that wasn't entirely true. Part of her craved his company. She knew very little about him but what she did know she liked. Another time, another place and she would have pulled out all the stops. Right now she knew she'd lost too many pounds except for her breasts and they seemed as full as they'd always been. Her hair needed trimming, she'd given up even minimal makeup and she desperately needed a manicure. But what was worse than her appearance was what Frankie thought of her character—she could hear it in his voice and see it in his eyes—and that was something she couldn't afford to repair.

"How is your grandmother?" he asked when she joined him on the porch.

"Seemingly content," Kate said, momentarily reliving the moment when she'd asked how much a week in that privately run home cost and been told a staggering amount. She tried not to reveal how devastating this news was. She was working hard to keep her grandmother from entering the state's care—which would require becoming a ward of the state and would mean her house would be lost. Juggling concern about her grandmother's state of mind, her health and money, too, was tricky. It required a positive outlook and that was a fight to maintain. Kate gripped the rail and faced the ever-present river running through the valley.

"Kate," Frankie said softly. "I want you to

know that you're welcome to stay on this ranch as long as you like. There's plenty of room and you cost next to nothing to feed."

She smiled. "I used to eat like a horse."

"Hard to believe. Anyway, while your grandmother is being cared for, maybe you could use this time to, I don't know, relax maybe."

"I thought summer was a busy time of year for you," she said.

"It is. But you don't need me to entertain you. You're an excellent horsewoman and knowing that your long-lost relatives came from this area, it might be fun to poke around. I mean once you make a decision about what you want to do about the documentary."

"So, if I support it, I can stay—"

"No," he said, shaking his head and smiling at her. "Don't go putting words in my mouth, that's not what I meant. No matter what you decide, you're welcome to stay here. That's all I'm trying to say."

"Are you people really as kind as you seem?" she asked.

"That's a strange question. The answer, I guess, is yes, in at least as much as we're pretty much exactly what you see."

She bit her lip. He was unwittingly offering her enough time to complete her search. "I do love the Bowline River." She sighed. "Well, thank you for the offer. Let's see what happens."

They walked toward the river, pausing at a bench Frankie told her Pike built a couple of years before. "Please, sit down," he said.

She did as he asked and he took a seat next to her. The bench was relatively small so this meant he was close enough to send a wave of warmth from his body to hers and she could not deny how good it felt.

By now it was twilight. The bench overlooked the river and the bridge below. Harry Hastings had said a previous bridge washed out a few years after the robbery. Where had the original been? As there was very little on this side of the river, it must have connected to a road that led up the opposing hill.

Was it possible she was looking too far upstream and on the wrong side of the river? She almost laughed—of course it was possible. The directions had been vague, at best. She found her gaze straying toward the far shore. Though it was more or less barren directly across from the house, she could see signs of heavy vegetation in the distance. A surge of hope made her breath catch.

At last Frankie spoke. "Who was Luke?" he asked. She snapped back into the moment. He immediately backpedaled. "I'm sorry. I didn't mean to ask that. It's none of my business."

"No, it isn't," she said. "But I'd like to tell you anyway."

Chapter Nine

"Luke Beckworth was a very nice guy who rented the house across the fence from my grandparents' place."

That's where she knew she should stop talking. Right there, not a word more. But she found she couldn't stop, partly because she was so relieved he hadn't asked about something she'd have to lie about but mostly because she wanted him to know.

"After Grandpa died, like I told you, Gram just lost it. It was a...well, an overwhelming time for me, too. I'd been this happy-go-lucky woman who did well in school, got my degree and a job teaching all in the same week. I loved Arizona. I had friends, hobbies, an apartment... you know, all the usual stuff people starting off have. And then the world just all changed, not just for my poor grandmother, but for me, too. She just started to disappear."

"It sounds lonely," Frankie said.

She nodded. "It was. And that's why when Luke started talking to me, I was so glad. After a while, I knew he cared more about me than I did him, so I told him we had to slow down. I didn't want to use him. He said he knew that I didn't love him the same way he loved me, but that I might someday if I just gave it time. I knew that was wishful thinking on his part. Love can grow, sure, but there has to be a spark and I just didn't feel it.

"He knew I was struggling, that Gram's house was falling apart and that I was doing my best to get it up to code. Anyway, he knew about the bills and the promises I'd made. He knew because I told him. I should never have done that. It was selfish of me…" Her voice trailed off. She couldn't stop now, though she knew in her heart that whatever misgivings Frankie had about her were going to get a lot worse.

"And then he came up with a plan he believed would ease my immediate worries," she continued. "He left Seattle and moved to Alaska to fish the snow crab season. He didn't tell me his plan face-to-face. Instead, he left me a note. He'd said he was going to make a lot of money and save every dime and give it to me. I knew he'd fished up there before, and I knew it was really dangerous work. I called him and told him to come back, that I wouldn't take his money, but he refused. He said if I wasn't so stressed-out, I could learn to love him. I tried to make him understand stress had nothing to do with my feelings, but he couldn't or wouldn't listen to me. In the end it didn't matter because within three weeks of starting that job, he was swept off the deck of the trawler and lost in the freezing sea. I as good as killed him."

She managed to get through this story dry-eyed for the simple reason she was too exhausted to shed another tear.

Frankie took her hands. "He was a grown man, Kate. He made his own decisions. Maybe his motives were misguided, but he sounds like a decent guy. Wouldn't he hate knowing his death weighs on your conscience?"

"Probably," she whispered.

"Come here," he said and pulled her against his side, his arm around her shoulders. "Maybe he was right," he said against her hair. "Maybe without all the worries, you would have been able to love him."

"No," she murmured as she inhaled the good, clean smell of his skin. She looked up at his shadowed face. The strong jaw, the hint of a beard, the tawny brown of his tanned skin, the contrasting whites of his eyes. She knew stress didn't stop attraction—indeed, she'd seldom been more stressed than right that moment, but Frankie still managed to draw her into his orbit. His lips were very close to hers. She recalled their earlier kiss with a haunting rush of desire and maybe that memory telegraphed on her face. The next thing she knew, he had lowered his lips to hers and this time she didn't hold back.

The last man she'd kissed with passion had been Luke, and it hadn't felt like this, not ever, not even when they made love. And she knew in her head it wasn't a matter of method or body parts or anything like that—it was feelings and passion that pulsed through her veins, that sparked the fire.

Because that's what it was: fire. Her whole body seemed to burst into flames and, as the kiss evolved, she grew increasingly heated until she had to break away to take a breath, to fall back to the scorched earth.

His phone rang at that moment and as it was still in Kate's pocket, she jumped in surprise. Frankie chuckled.

"Maybe it's about Gram," she said, fumbling in her pocket. She looked at the screen but it was the wrong area code. Fear had done a good job of dousing the inferno in which she'd been engulfed, but Frankie's arm still around her shoulders felt wonderful.

"I don't recognize this number," he said as

he took the phone from her hand. "I'd better answer it."

After a quick greeting, he talked for a few seconds and Kate tried not to listen, but he was too close for that.

"I see," he said. "Okay." He glanced at his watch. "I can meet you tonight. The Three Aces? Yeah, I know the joint. Say thirty minutes? Fine. See you then."

He clicked off the phone, pocketed it and kissed her forehead. "I have to go," he said. "There's someone I need to meet."

"Oh," she replied, intensely disappointed.

"Come with me."

She meant to decline. It was pretty clear to her that learning about Luke wasn't really the reason he'd asked her to take a walk, that he had another agenda and by going with him, she'd increase the opportunity he'd remember what it was. Better to refuse the invitation and go hide out in her room.

There was also another, equally compelling reason to stay behind. What in the world was the point of continuing this flirtation? But she heard herself agree to his request, and on some level understood that the point was being alive, the point was being Kate West, twenty-six-year-old woman for one more day, able to kiss a great-looking guy who made her insides flutter. There could be no other point.

She just needed to figure out why she couldn't stop spilling her guts to him!

As they drove up the main ranch road toward the highway he shot her a quick look. "You haven't even asked where we're going."

"I don't really care," she said.

"That somehow seems out of character."

"After going on and on about my sorry life—"

"Don't do that," he said gently. "Don't put yourself down. I think you're remarkable. But you have to know—we're meeting Sara, Dave Dalton's daughter."

"Oh, good," Kate said. Her heart went out to the poor woman; had she been in her place she, too, would have wanted to speak to the people who found her father's body. "Do you know what, exactly, she wants?"

"Not really," Frankie said, casting her a swift glance. "But I'm hoping she might know what it was her father was going to show me. I should warn you. The Three Aces can be a little on the raunchy side."

"It's been ages since I went into a raunchy bar," she said with a strange jolt of anticipation. "Bring it on."

THE TAVERN WAS CROWDED, noisy and dark. The air-conditioning barely functioned. Several men standing or sitting near the long, black bar greeted Frankie with slaps on the back and semiribald comments while eyeing Kate. Their gazes inevitably lingered on her breasts thanks to the snug T-shirt she'd changed into before dinner. It clung to every sumptuous curve; indeed, he'd been distracted by it all evening. He wanted to tell them to stop ogling her but that would just egg them on so he quietly led her away instead.

"Come here often?" Kate asked.

"Not anymore," Frankie said, omitting the fact that years before he'd called this place a second home and those guys at the bar his buddies. When he'd straightened out his life, he'd let destructive friendships lapse. Jay Thurman, the man he most dreaded seeing, wasn't here tonight; hopefully he was still serving time.

A solitary woman in her forties sat at a small table nursing a glass of red wine. "Sara?" Frankie asked as they paused in front of her.

"You must be Frank Hastings," she said with a tense smile. Her eyes were red-rimmed. "Please, sit down."

Frankie introduced Kate, as the waitress showed up at their table. He turned to Kate. "What would you like?"

"Iced tea would be fine," Kate said. Frankie ordered a draft beer, and the waitress left.

"You were there, too, weren't you?" Sara asked, gazing into Kate's eyes.

"Yes. I'm so sorry for your loss."

Sara tucked a strand of short black hair behind her ear as she ran a finger around the base of her glass. There was a hard edge to her appearance and a tendency to fall short of making eye contact. Frankie could not associate her with the man he'd seen swinging from the rafters.

"I had to see you," she began, "I have to know if you've remembered anything since yesterday that might help me understand what happened to Dad."

The waitress returned with their drinks and Frankie paid her. "I can't think of anything off the top of my head," he said. He was glad she'd shown up after the ambulance left. No child should have to see a parent in her father's ultimate condition. "Can you, Kate?"

"No," she said, lifting the tall glass to her lips.

"He had so much to live for," Sara added with a slight catch to her voice and a darted look that flicked away. "He loved retirement...he loved life."

"I had a good friend in college who committed suicide," Kate said gently. "It left everyone who knew her absolutely stunned, especially her family."

"You don't understand what I'm trying to

say," Sara protested. "I think someone killed my father."

Frankie had just taken a drink of frothy ale and it almost shot out of his mouth. He choked it down. "Have the police found some kind of evidence—"

"The police have insinuated I'm too upset to think clearly."

"What about the coroner?" Kate asked.

"His report says everything is consistent with a suicide."

"I take it they never found a note?" Frankie said.

"No. And that's because he didn't write one."

"I was under the impression he'd been dead for several days," Frankie said carefully. "When was the last time you spoke with him?"

"A week before the day you found him. He got off the phone when there was a knock on his door."

"Do you think that was his killer?" Kate asked, her blue eyes wide.

"I have no idea. We know what time the visitor knocked because the time and date of our call was still in his phone's memory, but we don't know who came to the door. You've been to his place, you've seen how remote the house is and how few neighbors he has… I can't find anyone who saw anything and neither can the sheriff's office. We're not positive exactly when he died."

"Can't forensics determine the time of death pretty accurately?" Kate asked.

"It was warm, the house was closed up, things…deteriorate faster. But you're right, they can get close. There just hasn't been time yet to finish all the tests."

"Did he have any enemies?" Frankie asked. "Anyone with a grudge?"

"No," she responded quickly. "I mean, he was a private guy but well respected. He drove a crane at a metal recycling plant for thirty-five years. Everyone liked him."

"So," Frankie said, striving to understand, "your conclusion that he didn't kill himself is based on a gut feeling?"

Again a direct look. "You say that like it's a bad thing, but it isn't. But that's not all. My dad was a methodical guy and he let something very important die with him. That's not like him."

"Something important? Like what?"

She paused and took another shallow breath. "I can't talk about it."

"Okay," Frankie said.

She stared at him for a second and sighed. "Oh, who am I kidding? You're not a police-man or anything, right?"

"Right," Frankie said and wondered what in the world Sara was struggling to say.

"I have to tell someone," she said. "There's no one else… My dad had something his father gave him. It should be mine now."

"What kind of thing?" Frankie asked.

She looked uncertain as she took a hasty sip of her wine.

"That's okay," Frankie said. "You don't have to tell us."

"Gold coins," she said so softly it was hard to hear her.

Frankie caught Kate's startled gaze.

"Every year or so, Dad would take some of these coins to this guy he knows in Boise who deals with things like that and he'd sell them," Sara continued. "He'd share the proceeds with me."

"Do you know where the coins came from?" Frankie asked.

"Not really, just that they'd been in the family. Dad hid them just like his father had. They came with the warning not to tell anyone about them and not to spend too many too fast because that would call unwanted attention. And then he just clammed up. I begged him to tell me where he'd stashed them in case he died or something, but he just wouldn't. Still, he wouldn't have killed himself without telling me where he put them."

"What about a safe-deposit box or—"

"He didn't have one. He didn't trust banks."

"He was going to show me something," Frankie said quietly, looking around the tavern, trying to see if any of his former pals were paying any attention to this conversation. They didn't seem to be. "That's why I went to his house yesterday. I'm doing a documentary about stolen coins from a bank robbery a hundred years ago. Your father's name came up as a descendent of a man who used to live in this town, a man named Matthew Dalton."

"He was a long-distant relative of mine, right?"

"Yeah. He moved out of Green Ridge soon after the robbery back in 1915."

"That's right, now I remember. I've forgotten a lot of the details. He was Dad's great-grandfather. I think that's what it was, anyway. I seem to recall he married a local girl. I can't remember her name. Mary, maybe. Dad could have told you more."

"We have an historian working with us," Frankie said, "so we know Matthew Dalton died five years after he left these parts. His widow was a younger woman named Mary and they had two children, a little boy named George who was born to Matthew's first wife, and a girl named Amelia who Mary gave birth to. I was hoping your dad would have additional information. See, one of the robbers got away with a bag of gold."

"Gold? In what form?"

"Coins."

She opened her mouth and closed it quickly. After a minute or so, she leaned across the table. "Are you saying that Matthew Dalton robbed a bank? That Dad's gold is from that robbery? Wasn't Matthew Dalton an attorney? That doesn't sound like a bank robber to me."

"I agree. We know his first wife died when he overturned their carriage and that was a good year before he left Green Ridge with his second wife and his infant son, George. His left leg was crushed in the accident and he lost part of it. I guess he lived in constant pain."

"He doesn't sound like a prime suspect, does he?" Kate asked.

"No," Frankie said.

"And he died impoverished," Sara added. "That's what I always heard. If he had access to gold, why wouldn't he have used it to support his family?"

Frankie shrugged. "Still, the coincidence of his great-grandson inheriting a stash of secret gold coins is pretty startling. I'd sure like to see one."

"So would I," Sara said. "I have no idea where they are. Or the letter."

"There was a letter?"

"Yeah. Written by a woman. Dad didn't tell me who she was."

"Maybe he was going to show me the letter," Frankie mused. He thought for a second before adding, "Who inherits his estate?"

"Me," Sara said.

"But why have you told us all this?" Kate said softly.

"I can't find the coins. I thought maybe you would remember something that would help me figure out who wanted him dead. I have to find out if his killer stole them."

"I'm sorry, but I can't think of anything," Frankie said.

"I figured it was a long shot," Sara said, as she looked around the room then back at him. "I had to try something."

They sat in silence for a moment before Frankie cleared his throat. "Sara, would you be willing to tell me the name of the coin dealer? He was the only other person who knew about your father's treasure, wasn't he?"

"He knew about the coins, but Dad wouldn't have shared details," she said suddenly. "Maybe he guessed, though."

"Can you tell the police what you've told us?"

"No," she said firmly. "I promised my father I wouldn't tell anyone and I'm not going to break that promise. Except I already did. I told you two."

"We're not going to blab about it," Frankie said. "If those coins are from the robbery, there's no saying who really owns them now. What if I go see this coin dealer? Maybe he still has one of the coins and I could at least examine it and maybe sound him out about your dad."

"I guess that would be okay," Sara said.

"To ease your mind a little, we've recently had news that there's a good chance the stolen gold is still buried near the old town. In that case, your coins came from somewhere else. And one more thing," he added, "If you ever find the letter, would you let me read it?"

"Yes, of course. The coin dealer's name is Ed Hoskins. That's all I know about him." She drained her glass and rose. "I have to get back. I have a funeral to plan."

Chapter Ten

"This is your night for eliciting confidences, isn't it?" Kate said as they drove over the cattle grate onto Hastings land. "First me, then Sara."

"It's been quite an evening," he said.

"What did you make of Sara's story?"

"I think she believes her father was murdered," he said, "but that doesn't mean it's true. And I have to wonder why she was willing to tell us about the gold but won't tell the police."

"Well, we have no way to take it from her," Kate said. "They could."

"We could bop her over the head or talk about it to others and one of them could go after it. Trust me, there's no lack of people in this world anxious to line their pockets with another person's treasure."

He finished that statement with a strange undertone in his voice that she was momentarily too distracted to investigate. The comment had hit a little close to home. "Fear can push people in strange directions," she finally said.

"Or guilt," he said. "Or greed. Or just plain stupidity. The list goes on."

They drove a half mile or so before Kate gestured at a road leading off at a right angle toward the hillside. "Where do all these roads go?"

"That one goes to Pike's house," he said.

"And all the others?"

"Chance's place, equipment barns, hay storage, distant pastures, a water tank, old sheep pens, pump houses, loading gates…here and there."

Kate studied his profile as he spoke. The evening seemed to have brought them closer and that was a double-edged sword if there ever was one. "You might be an uncle by now," she said, suddenly remembering Kinsey and wondering how she was doing.

"I hope so," he said. "I adored Gerard's first daughter. Do you know about her and her mom?"

"Yes. Kinsey mentioned them this morning."

"What a tragedy. But look what he managed to rebuild for himself. You never know about life, do you?"

"I guess not," Kate said. "But sometimes it seems like nothing is ever going to change, even though in your head you know that's not true. Everything changes."

"That's why you can't give up," Frankie said and there was an odd tone to his voice.

"You sound as if you have some experience with that," she mused.

He flashed her a quick smile. "Thanks to my misspent youth. Anyway, did you know Grace is Dad's seventh wife?"

"Seven!"

"All my brothers and I have different mothers. Dad started early and until Grace came along, his love life was a revolving door. I think all four of his sons have vowed not to recreate his pattern. We've all been very careful about choosing the right people—well, they have at least, but that's my plan, as well. I'd like my kids to all have the same parents."

As an only child, Kate had never really given this much thought. From where she stood now, which was pretty much alone, having siblings looked like a wonderful thing no matter who their parents were. She suspected Frankie was very lucky that he and all his brothers had had the option to stay with their dad so they grew up in the same house.

They passed a spur off to their left with a keep-off sign dangling from a chain across the road. He drove on about twenty feet, stopped the truck and looked across the gear shift console and straight into her eyes. "You in any rush?"

A little voice in her head chanted at her not to extend her time alone with him. Like every other warning her conscious mind tried offering when it came to Frankie, she ignored it. "No," she said.

He backed up. Then he got out of the truck without saying a word, took down the chain, drove the truck through and got out to replace the chain.

Still with no explanation, they rambled along a dirt road for a while, the headlights picking up increasing signs of forestation. Kate wondered what was going on but as she was pretty sure this road paralleled the river and might actually be taking her where she planned to sneak off to by herself tomorrow, she stayed quiet and tried to decipher landmarks in the dark. When through a gap in the trees she noticed a light flashing high above the river on the opposite shore and at some distance, she gestured at it. "What's that?"

"Radio tower on top of Mt. Jinx. Mt. Jinx is the location of the old gold mine located in Green Ridge."

"Is that its real name?"

"No. People just started calling it that when two miners died in separate accidents a week apart. On the survey maps, it's referred to as Green Peak."

As he turned a curve, Kate caught a glimpse of moonlight on water flowing down below. After that, all she could discern in the headlamps was an ever thickening grove of fir trees. And when he turned off the ignition, even they disappeared.

"Let's get out," he said and she saw the whites of his teeth as he smiled.

"Okay, you've got me curious," she said as they stood together in a small clearing. Moonlight had a hard time penetrating the trees. "Why are we here? What is this place?"

He took her hand. "Follow me," he said and led her deeper into the trees along a wide trail he was obviously so familiar with he could walk it in the dark. Debris crunched under their feet. The air smelled woodsy and clean and she inhaled deeply as the cool air bathed her face. She liked the feel of Frankie's strong hand holding hers, the warmth that spread through her fingers. He finally stopped and put an arm around her.

She all but vibrated with the anticipation of the touch of his lips against hers, the desire to be in his arms, to feel his body pressed against her, his hands on her skin.

"Look up," he whispered against her forehead. In the same instant she heard a soft click, a hundred tiny lights flashed on in the trees above.

"Oh, my gosh," Kate gasped. "What's up there?"

"I'll show you," he said as he pocketed a small remote. Thanks to the lights now twinkling above, she could see a spiral ramp encircling one of the tall fir trees, leading up into the branches. Still clutching Kate's hand, Frankie started climbing and she followed.

Around and around the tree they climbed until they stepped onto a railed deck that surrounded the small building constructed using the tree as its anchor. Frankie opened a door and flicked another switch on his remote. Two hanging lantern type lamps immediately sprang to life, revealing a circular room with a roof made of varnished boards rising to a peak. The small building was set up with an efficient kitchen including a gas stove and a table with two chairs, a bed, a small chest and shelves of books. Pictures hung on the walls and a built-in desk occupied a small alcove.

"I can't believe this," Kate said looking around in wonder. "It's absolutely beautiful. Did you build it yourself?"

"Yeah," he said.

"So this is your retreat?"

"That's right. I've been working on it for years. There's a generator located downstairs but I don't use it unless I plan to spend a good amount of time here. The damn thing makes a racket and I like the peace and quiet of the forest."

As he spoke, he walked around the room and pulled on dangling cords that raised bamboo blinds over windows allowing the outside lights to shine indoors. Kate walked over to peer outside. One window turned out to be a door with a glass panel leading to a walkway covered with more lights. It traveled nine or ten feet to the trunk of another tree where it connected to the beginnings of another platform. "I'm starting stage two of the house later this summer when things slow down around here."

"How many stages do you plan on?"

"Three. Eventually, this will be the living room, the next tree over will be the kitchen, and the last will be a bedroom."

"What about the family you mentioned wanting?"

He smiled. "That's a long time away."

She looked around again. "I can't believe this place. I have a little experience pounding nails, but this is something else."

"I like construction. My brothers built their houses, as well. We all pitched in to help each other."

"Did they take part in creating this masterpiece?"

"No, this one I wanted to do alone. I'm not sure if anyone knows it's back here. I've tried to keep it private, but knowing my family, who knows? I suspect some of them might figure I'm not always off causing trouble when I disappear for a few days at a time. I haven't announced it, though. It's a little fanciful for most cowboys' taste."

"I love it," she said, looking up at the high ceiling. Between the gold of the wood and the oranges and yellows of the materials covering the floor-bound mattress, it had an *Arabian Nights* kind of feeling. Warm, she thought, like its builder. She sat down on the mattress, her arms around her bent legs.

"You look beautiful in this soft light," he said as he sat down beside her.

She smiled. "Frankie, why did you bring me here if it's your private space?"

He raised a hand and touched her hair. "I'm not sure," he said.

"Is it because I told you about Luke? Did you want to share something with me because I shared something with you?"

He studied her face for a moment. "Maybe."

She leaned toward him and touched her lips to his. "I had to do that," she said a moment later. "I've been wishing you'd kiss me since the minute we got out of your truck."

"I've wanted to," he said, "but it seemed kind of presumptuous for me to show you my house with this nice big mattress and then make a pass."

"Good point."

"There's something else I've wanted to do all night," he added.

"And what is that?"

He clicked off the lamps and the room turned into the interior of a magical, woodsy globe, the smell of fir and nature vying with his own masculine scent to drive her crazy. He raised his hands and reached around her head. The next thing she knew, he'd loosened the band that held her braid in place, releasing her heavy blond mane. He ran his fingers through the waves, bringing her hair around to fall beside her face where he smoothed it with his hands. At last he cupped her cheeks.

Staring into her eyes, he whispered, "You have the most exquisite face I've ever seen." And then he kissed her, and if she'd thought the kiss up by the house had created a firestorm, it was nothing compared to what happened this time.

She had a few seconds to think how far she was willing to let this go. She'd not had a whole bunch of lovers in her life and while she'd been fond of every one of them, none had touched her as deeply, affected her as completely. His hot breath fanned her neck as he rained kisses on her throat, and physical sensations soon overwhelmed the emotions she'd been dealing with since the moment he first said her name.

"Tell me when to stop," he whispered against her ear, and with that drew her down to lie on the bed beside him.

She'd known him only three days but his body stretched beside hers felt familiar and good. Three days though…and three miserable lying days they'd been. He thought she was one kind of woman and she knew she was another. Making love to him was not only premature but likely to lead to hurt and pain for both of them.

It took her several minutes of battling desire with willpower before she found the strength to take his hands from her breasts and hold them in hers. By then, she was half-undressed and shaking with desire. So was he. Climbing down off the tower of passion they'd built proved as treacherous as descending a mountain during avalanche season. But he seemed to understand her unspoken message and gradually their kisses grew less intense until he held her in his arms and they both lay staring up at the twinkling lights dancing across the floor and walls as the breeze outside stirred the wires that held them.

"I'm glad you're staying here longer," he whispered. "I couldn't stand it if you left tomorrow."

She peered into his eyes but didn't say a word. The truth was she felt exactly the same way.

The potential for disaster loomed like an angry grizzly, baring its teeth and growling a warning she knew she'd probably ignore.

Chapter Eleven

Frankie drove Kate back to the ranch and kissed her in the moonlight as the three ranch dogs milled about their legs. He hadn't asked her about her exploits on the river and he no longer wanted to. He didn't want to spy on her, either. If Pat Lowell said she was okay then she was okay and the thought he might distance her before he knew her well enough to establish a bond was too much to bear, especially after the last hour.

She felt like she belonged in his arms and, face it, he could not wait to consummate their relationship. After hearing about her involvement with Luke, however, he could see where he would need to be patient.

Patience had never really been one of his virtues; on the other hand, he had learned a little restraint and he'd also learned that acting rashly could have dire consequences. And when exactly was he going to share his past with her?

Later, he decided. Not tonight. Tonight was his to tuck away. It was a beginning, he could feel it in his bones. There was something unique and special about Kate.

He said good-night to her at the door and that felt weird. "You're not coming in?" she asked.

"No. I'm going back to the tree."

"Why?"

"I'll dream better there," he said and laughed at how silly it sounded. "Truth is I don't trust myself to sleep in the same house with you."

KATE FOUND LILY standing in front of the stove dressed in a robe and slippers. Lily gestured at the small saucepan on the burner. "My mom swore warm milk helped her sleep. Time to put it to the test."

"You're having trouble sleeping?" Kate asked.

"Yeah. Kinsey is still at the hospital. I haven't heard anything for an hour or two."

"I've heard labor can last a long time," Kate said.

"I know. I just have a special place in my heart for Kinsey and Gerard and I want everything to be perfect for them."

"Frankie said you and Chance are engaged."

"Yes," Lily said with a smile as she poured

the steaming milk into a mug. "Have you met him yet?"

"No. I haven't met him or Gerard. Are they a lot like Frankie?"

"Not really. For four men raised in the same house, they all have their differences. Frankie and Chance were the hellions when they were younger. But they turned out really well. You never know."

Kate laughed. "I guess so."

Lily's voice grew soft. "Charlie is just crazy about Chance. And Chance is fabulous with Charlie. We're getting married in September and neither one of us can wait to have another child. When I look at where my life was a year ago and where it is now—well, I owe it all to Chance and the Hastings family."

"You're happy," Kate said.

"Yes." Lily tasted her cup of milk and made a face. "Bleech!"

"My grandmother likes warm milk, too," Kate said. "It never did much for me."

"I know how to fix it," Lily said, and took a bottle of chocolate syrup out of the fridge. She squeezed in a dollop and stirred. "Better," she said after a sip. "Okay, I'll try again. 'Night."

"Good night," Kate said but she stood there in the darkened room for a few moments. Why was she suddenly so anxious? Had some of Lily's concerns about Kinsey rubbed off?

Maybe her tightly stretched nerves had more to do with concerns about her own tumultuous life and talk about grandmothers than it did any real fear for Kinsey. Kate picked the phone off the counter and called Seattle. Pine Hill assured her Gram was asleep.

Kate walked back to the little bedroom and sat on the bed. Her backpack was in the closet, out of sight, but she could feel it calling, reminding her tomorrow was a new day, and she had another stretch of river to search.

She wanted the comfort of Frankie's arms and cursed herself for running away from him tonight. She wanted to be beside him in his bed. She wanted his warmth and strength to push everything else away.

Was that using him? Was she falling into the same trap she'd fallen into with Luke? Was she comforting herself at someone else's expense?

The questions had no direct answers but she suspected comparing her feelings for these two men was as useless as comparing the men. They were different people with different qualities. Luke had offered uncomplicated comfort, at least at first. Frankie did not. He was as stimulating as he was relaxing, just as scary as compassionate. And so sexy that even thinking about him made her steaming hot.

Would he welcome her back?

There was one way to find out.

She left the house and walked toward the barn. The dogs kept her company as she saddled a horse, the red one again, and took off. She rode over the moonlit bridge and down the main road until she reached the chain and the Keep Out sign. Leaving it in place, she maneuvered the mare around the post that supported one end of the chain and trotted down the road.

She found the clearing and got off the horse, leading her down the path a few steps but stopping short when she smelled cigarette smoke.

Did Frankie smoke? She'd inhaled his scent many times that evening and without exception had found it as clean and refreshing as running water. He must have a visitor, but it surprised her he would allow someone to smoke that close to the tree that held his home.

She stayed where she was, unsure what to do, listening for voices. Meeting someone out here was totally unexpected but how could she say that? She was the stranger around these parts. This could be one of Frankie's brothers or his father. Did she want them knowing she had come to pay a midnight visit?

Nope.

But how did they get here? There'd been no vehicle where Frankie parked. More to the point, how did she get away without them hearing her and the horse move? A minute later, she heard a deep cough and she peered through the underbrush to glimpse the dark shape of a man twice as bulky as Frankie. He coughed into his hand again—a smoker's cough—then swore. The shape lumbered toward her, heavy steps breaking twigs on the forest floor. Her heart lodged in her throat and she willed the horse to stay silent. A car door opened, which shocked the shoes off her—she hadn't anticipated anyone would drive on the path.

The interior lights illuminated the pale, jowly face of a man in his midthirties. He heaved his bulk into the car and closed the door.

She immediately moved off the path.

The only Hastings brothers she hadn't met were Chance and Gerard and if that man was either one of them, she'd eat her saddle. All the Hastings men she'd seen were tall and fit, bronzed and honed by hard work. They all bore more than passing similarities. But this guy, so briefly glimpsed, had left a lasting impression of pasty skin and a shifty tilt to his eyes. It appeared he hadn't shaved in days.

She heard the car start but the headlights did not go on. The path must be a lot wider than she'd thought when she walked it in the dark with Frankie. For a second, she wondered why he hadn't driven all the way in to the tree, but then she thought she knew. Approaching it on foot, holding hands…it had enhanced the magic and the thrill of discovery. It had been a gift and she smiled with the warmth of the memory.

Lights still off, the car moved closer to Frankie's tree until she heard the creak of brakes. A flash of illumination announced the driver had once again gotten out. A moment later, headlights and engine noises came from behind her. Someone else was coming. She pulled the horse off the path and a second later, Frankie's truck passed her by—he was home and the mere fact he'd arrived calmed her.

But why in the world was Frankie meeting someone in this way? He'd made it sound like his home was a sanctuary, a secret even, and yet here was this man, waiting for him in the dark. The only thing that made sense to her was that Frankie didn't know what was coming and that made her anxious.

Good sense demanded she turn around right that moment and head back to the barn. But good sense couldn't battle the powerful pull of curiosity or her growing unease. When she heard

Frankie's engine turn off, she tied the horse to a branch and sneaked forward on her own.

"About time you got back," a low, gruff voice boomed.

"Who's there?" Frankie demanded. The small lights in the tree flashed on and she heard Frankie's sharp intake of breath. "Jay? Jay Thurman?"

"In the flesh, buddy."

"Are you smoking?"

"So what if I am."

Kate had adjusted herself to see through the branches. "This is a damn forest, you idiot," Frankie said as he grabbed the cigarette from Jay's mouth and stubbed it out with his boot. "I thought you were still doing time," he added.

Jay's laugh held no mirth. "What would you know about doing time? You're the golden boy with the rich father and the Get Out of Jail Free card. You sold me right smack down the river. I got out a week ago and, funny thing, all I could think about was renewing our…friendship."

"We were never friends," Frankie scoffed. "You used me."

"We used each other. But I paid the whole bill and you got off scot-free."

"I didn't get off scot-free," Frankie said, his voice low now. She could hear the anger boiling underneath the words.

"I figure you owe me," Jay continued.

"How did you find this place?" Frankie demanded.

"I've been hanging out at The Three Aces every night. I knew you'd show up eventually and tonight was the night. I followed you back here. You were so struck on that little gal, you didn't even notice. You two looked mighty cozy up there on that nice, soft bed. It's been a while since I had a woman. Maybe I could borrow her."

"Get out of here," Frankie said. "And don't talk about her again."

"Touchy, touchy. But I ain't going nowhere."

"Get on with it, Jay. What do you want?"

There was a long pause before Jay spoke again. "I wonder how your old man would feel about you if he knew the truth."

"If that's all you've got to say—"

"No, that's not all. I've got a proposition."

"What kind of proposition?"

"Not here, not now," Jay said after a minute.

"Then when and where?"

"Tomorrow night at The Three Aces. Ten o'clock. That'll give you time to imagine the fallout if I'm...forced...to speak my mind. I'd show up if I were you."

"Just get out of here."

Jay laughed. "Sure, boss. Anything you say."

Kate heard the car door again, then the engine gunned and the car lurched backward. She kneeled down in the bushes and hoped the man didn't look forward until her horse was out of sight. She didn't take a deep breath until she heard the car screech and groan and eventually speed away.

She lifted a foot, every instinct in her body urging her to run to Frankie, to offer support to ask what all this meant.

He'd disappeared from view, but seconds later she heard a muffled oath and then footfalls as he climbed the ramp.

How could she ask for an explanation? Couldn't he demand the same thing from her? She waited until the slam of the door in the tree high above her rang in the night air, then she turned and trotted back to the mare.

Who was Jay Thurman and what truth did Frankie fear him exposing?

Chapter Twelve

To Frankie's surprise, Grace was back in the kitchen when he arrived at five in the morning. His dad was at the table tucking into bacon and eggs.

"Can I make you a plate?" Grace asked him.

"No thanks," he said and realized at once how impatient he sounded. He showed her the thermos. "I came to bum some coffee to take out to the combine."

"Of course," she said.

"Where'd you spend the night?" Harry asked.

"I've asked you not to ask me that," Frankie said.

His father laughed. "It's okay, I was young once, too."

Frankie knew what his father assumed and he ignored the wink that went with the comment. Instead he addressed Grace. "Do we have a baby yet?"

"No," she replied as she handed him the full thermos. "Kinsey came home in the wee hours of the morning. No baby. They said it was false labor. Surely it can't go on much longer, can it? She was due over a week ago."

"You were a nurse," Frankie said. "I daresay you know a lot more about this than I do." His gaze traveled down the hall toward the back of the house.

"She's not up yet," Grace said.

He was on the verge of asking Grace what she meant, but he stopped himself from acting the idiot. "Will you tell her I'll be back at noon so we can ride out to see the ghost town?"

"You still haven't made it there? Isn't she leaving early tomorrow morning?"

"I don't think so. Her house flooded and her grandmother is in a home for a week so she has a little extra time here. I assume that's okay?"

"Of course it is," Grace said. "The girl is no problem at all."

"Kind of a loner, isn't she?" Frankie's father said.

Frankie shrugged. "Kind of. Thanks for the coffee," he told them and left the house, disappointed not to have even glimpsed Kate and yet relieved, too.

The conversation—if that's what last night's discussion with Jay Thurman could be called—

had peppered his sleep with random dreams. And when he'd woken up, as he had off and on all night, every noise became Jay coming back to taunt him...or worse. The fact he'd seen Kate with Frankie was worrisome, as well. He didn't want that animal anywhere near her.

How ironic that the one man in the world he least wanted to know his exact location now knew it. How had he driven home without noticing he was being tailed? The main road was easy to explain...there had been traffic last night and he'd been full of thoughts about Sara's conviction her father was killed and the information about those mysterious gold coins. A tail was the last thing on his mind. You would have thought he would have spotted Jay's car once they got to the ranch, though, but by then he and Kate were talking and Jay must have switched off his headlights. Somehow he'd seen Frankie use the turn-off and from what he said, he'd even looked through a window.

That was a sobering thought.

Jay was a loose cannon, a wild, impetuous man with a violent temper and a mean streak a mile wide. Tonight had vanquished any hope he might have changed.

Frankie had been a fool to get involved with him ten years before. As it was, the experience had taught him some hard life lessons, but those had come with his father's loss of respect, which Frankie had worked years to reestablish. He felt he finally had it—the thought Jay could ruin this made his gut twist. And it wouldn't be just his father, either—his brothers, the women who lived on the ranch and now, Kate, too.

Secrets could start out innocent or self-serving, but so many of them grew exponentially in the dark recesses of their habitats, exacting a high price in the end. Jay's silence was also going to cost—Frankie didn't know how much, but he knew money would be involved. He hoped he had enough to satisfy the guy. No way was he borrowing from family or friends. And how did you take a loan from a bank to cover blackmail?

KATE MET FRANKIE at noon. He seemed distracted but maybe that was just the spin she put on his curt manner since she knew what had happened the night before. She looked deep into his gray eyes and for the first time since she'd met him, he broke the connection.

It wasn't her imagination.

They rode in silence, which was okay with Kate as she'd spent the morning searching the shoreline of the river on the southwestern side of the current bridge and had a lot to think about. She'd been told that the site she sought existed within a mile of that bridge. She'd pretty much exhausted possibilities northeast of there, but then she groaned. She hadn't looked on the southeast side of the river because she'd had things turned around in her head. It suddenly seemed a daunting task. Everything would need to be repeated on the opposite shore and farther west. She wished she could confide in Frankie and ask for help.

A dozen times that afternoon, the words almost left her lips but she always swallowed them whole.

The ghost town turned out to be fascinating in its own way and she wished they'd come before Frankie's mood took a nosedive. She could see why it fascinated him. He told her why some of the buildings were burned—the fire that had killed Lily's husband was responsible for that. He also pointed out the collapsed roof of another building—that's where Gerard's first wife and daughter died.

"This place really is filled with ghosts," she said as they walked down the street.

"That's the bank," he said, pointing at a faded building on the corner whose top floor seemed to have fallen in on itself.

"Are all the original buildings here?"

"No. Some were private homes that disappeared a long time ago."

She looked around. The structures on the main street seemed to huddle together to support each other like a very old, very feeble family who had fallen on hard times.

"The place is too decrepit and too structurally damaged to repair," he continued. "After we shoot this documentary, we're going to raze it. It presents too much of a hazard and probably should have been done decades ago."

"I'm beginning to see why it captures your imagination," she told him as they wound up at the old mine. A new-looking barrier appeared to be bolted over the entrance.

"I can see people walking these streets," he said. "I can imagine them going to the mercantile and the bank. The saloon must have been hopping on paydays. People lived and died, loved and laughed, cried and longed for better days, all right here on these streets, inside these buildings."

She loved it when he talked this way and looked up at him. They'd shared a special hour together the night before but it was over. She couldn't help feeling a piercing stab of regret.

"So what do you think?" he asked as they walked back down the street.

She longed to assure him she wouldn't stand in the way of the documentary. Eventually, he would probably discover their historian had been wrong about her claims and wow, would he detest her then. As if to protect herself a little longer, she wanted his approval now, she wanted to see him smile, to be happy.

But in his current state, might not the news that he needn't worry about her trying to stop the film cause him to hasten her on her way? She had a gut feeling that despite earlier blunders, she would find the spot she sought and uncover the treasure that would help her fulfill her promise to her grandfather. She couldn't take that risk.

"I'll have an answer for you by tomorrow night," she said.

He stopped dead in his tracks and stared down at her. She could tell his bad mood was pushing him over the top. "Frankie—"

"You just like keeping me on the hook, don't you?"

"No, I—"

"After last night, I'd think you'd care more about…this."

"Last night?" she said. "Is that why you took me to your tree house? Is that why you kissed me?"

"You kissed me first," he said.

"No, you kissed me when we sat on the bench."

"Yeah," he said. "That's right, when we sat by the river. The river you can't take your eyes off.

The river that fascinates you to the point—" He bit off his own words and stared at her, then he grabbed her upper arms and pulled her to him. His kiss was provoking in a way that pushed blood through her body like a fire hose. After an all-encompassing second or two, she pulled herself together, broke their connection and raised her hand to slap him.

He caught her wrist. "Come off it," he said.

"I never would have thought this of you," she whispered.

"That's because you don't know me."

"I thought I did."

"In three days? That's enough time to know you're hot for someone, not enough to..."

"To what?"

"To...care."

"Man, you are all over the map, aren't you? What's going on?"

"Nothing," he said. "Maybe you'd like to tell me what's going on with you. Why you lug that backpack around and why—"

His ringing phone cut him off midsentence.

"Yeah," he barked into the phone, listened a minute and shook his head. When he spoke again, he'd modified his voice. "Thanks for calling me back, Mr. Hoskins. I'd like to talk to you about gold coins. May I make an appointment to visit your store?"

That had to be Dave Dalton's coin-dealing contact. At least Frankie could talk civil to a stranger. The thought seemed to telegraph to his head from hers and he turned his back on her and stepped away.

"Your place is in Boise, right?

"Oh, I see. May I ask where?" He paused as if listening to another question.

"It's important," he said as though Hoskins was dragging his feet. "No, sir, today would be better." Silence continued and then Frankie took a deep breath. "That's great. No, actually, that's closer than Boise. In about two hours? Thanks." He switched off the phone. When he turned around to face Kate, he all but winced.

"Kate—"

"I gather Mr. Hoskins will talk to you?"

"Thank goodness he called."

"That coin is really important to you, isn't it?"

"Yes, but that's not why I'm thankful. It stopped me from making more of a jerk of myself. I need to apologize for my behavior."

"Let's just forget it, okay?" she said. He'd been getting awfully close to uncomfortable territory when the call came. She was not anxious to resume their conversation.

He stepped closer to her. "I don't have any excuses to offer," he said. "I wouldn't blame you if you left right now and started the biggest internet campaign the world has ever seen. All I can tell you is that I have another issue that's making me nuts and I took everything out on you."

"I understand," she said, wishing with all her heart they could just speak the things that needed to be said. He leaned down and kissed her forehead. "I did not take you home last night to seduce you in order to get your cooperation with the documentary. I don't expect you to believe me—"

"But I do believe you," she said. "Or at least I want to."

"I don't need a reason to try to seduce you," he said as his fingers brushed against her face. "The fact is I'm crazy about you. I know it sounds nuts."

She didn't trust herself to speak. Her throat had closed off for a second and her heart drummed against her ribs. He was crazy about her—the feeling was mutual.

"I wish we'd met under different circumstances," he continued. "At a different time in both of our lives."

"I do, too," she said and stepped into his arms. He kissed her gently as though in apology for his earlier effort and she closed her eyes. For several moments, they stood together in the middle of the old town. If the ghosts lurked nearby, they at least had the decency to remain hidden.

"Let's just get through the next day," she said. "Then we'll go back to our regular lives and maybe someday—"

"Someday?"

"When things are better, when we're, well, free. Or at least when I'm free. I know you are now except for the documentary…" She stopped talking because his eyebrows had arched and she realized she was rambling.

"Do you want to come with me to see Hoskins?"

Of course she did. "No," she finally muttered. "I really am exhausted."

He cupped her face, stared into her eyes and smiled. "Maybe a walk by the river would help you relax."

"Maybe so," she said, doing her best not to read too much into his words, but that smile… no, he didn't know exactly what she was up to but he wasn't an idiot and she hadn't exactly been subtle. The day after tomorrow, she'd be gone. This would all be over, and he would be a fond memory and nothing more and what he thought of her wouldn't matter. The important thing was that no one would ever know what she found—if she found it.

Although they chatted a little on the way back to the ranch, it was almost a relief when

Frankie drove off the ranch and she could return to the river. This afternoon she would rule out the south side across from the area where she'd searched the day before. The shore there wasn't wooded, but so much time had passed, nothing could be taken for granted. And then tomorrow, she'd start in on the riverfront down the hill from Frankie's tree.

Time was running out.

Chapter Thirteen

Ed Hoskins lived almost as much in the middle of nowhere as Frankie did. His property was heavily fenced—actually more like barricaded. An electronic gate was accompanied with an intercom while two security cameras focused on the driveway. Frankie flipped a button on the intercom and a moment later, the voice he recognized from the phone came on the line.

"Is that you, Mr. Hastings?" the man said.

"It is."

"Are you armed?"

"No, sir, I'm not. Should I be?"

Hoskins chuckled. "I'll buzz you through."

For all the security, the house itself was a modest brick structure with a steep tin roof and iron grills over all the windows. Hoskins opened the door before Frankie could turn off the engine. He scanned the yard as though checking to make sure no one had come through the gate on Frankie's heels.

"May I see identification?" Hoskins asked when Frankie reached the door.

Frankie took out his wallet and handed it to Hoskins who made a point of studying Frankie's picture. As he did that, Frankie perused Hoskins. He found a short, plump guy with a flamboyant black mustache several shades darker than the gray ringing his head. Bushy eyebrows settled on top of wire-framed glasses. A pair of jaunty red suspenders kept his slacks from slipping down under his round belly.

"Come inside," Hoskins said and made a last hasty search of the fenced yard before closing the door and sliding home the dead bolt.

All this security remained a mystery to Frankie as he noted the details of the sparsely outfitted room: two chairs flanking a gas fireplace, television, area rug, stereo and a bookcase. Through an open arch he could see a small utility kitchen. A narrow door opened off the opposite wall but it was closed.

"You've got this place set up like Fort Knox," Frankie commented.

Hoskins chuckled again. "I like feeling safe."

"Is your store in Boise equally secure?"

"Of course," he said. He gestured at a set of wing back chairs. "Have a seat," he said and settled into one himself. Frankie sat down, as well. "Now tell me, what kind of gold coin are you looking for?"

Frankie took a deep breath, sat forward a little and planted his hands on his bent knees. He hadn't mentioned Dalton's name on the phone lest he scare Hoskins off but there was no reason to pussyfoot around it now. "I'm looking for a coin like those Dave Dalton sold you."

"Dave Dalton?" Hoskins mused as though trying to place the name.

"Dave is dead," Frankie added.

The bushy eyebrows bunched together. "How unfortunate for the poor man. Might I ask how he died?"

"The police are calling it suicide. His daughter thinks he was murdered and we're both wondering if his stash of gold coins is the reason."

Hoskins stared at him for a moment before saying, "Why aren't the police talking to me?"

"Because his daughter doesn't want to reveal the existence of the coins to authorities."

"Why are you here, then?"

Frankie explained about the 1915 robbery and his determination to record the events on film before what remained of the ghost town disappeared forever.

"I know about the robbery, of course," Hoskins said. "To my knowledge, the gold was never recovered. I didn't know about the documentary. Fascinating."

"There's reason to believe most or all of the robbery loot is still buried on or near our family's ranch. We'll know soon."

"Then why do you wish to discuss this coin?"

Frankie explained about Dalton's connection to the town. "It strikes me as awfully coincidental. All I really need to know is what kind of coin it is and when and where it was minted. I can't prove a thing about who it belongs to. That's not my interest. But if we find the rest of the coins and this one is similar it raises additional questions. Dalton's daughter should be aware of that possibility. If the coins Dalton sold you were minted after the robbery, then this avenue of speculation could be closed."

Hoskins still hadn't admitted any involvement and Frankie was beginning to think he never would. Was it possible Dalton had misled his daughter to protect the true identity of his real contact?

"You had a run-in with the law," Hoskins said with one raised eyebrow.

Frankie was snapped from his thoughts. "A long time ago," he said.

"Thanks to the information age nothing is a long time ago anymore. It's still a matter of pub-

lic record and information about it appears when
your name is entered into a search engine."

"I did community service," Frankie said quietly. For years he hadn't dwelled on the idiocy
of his youth and no one had mentioned it. Now,
twice within a twenty-four-hour period, it was
back. Maybe he needed to work on his karma.
"I didn't actually go to jail," he added.

"Hmm." Hoskins steepled his fingers and
held them against his lips as he stared into
Frankie's eyes. "It would seem you've mended
your ways," he said.

"I have sincerely attempted to do just that,"
Frankie said. "Why are you bringing this up?
What's it to you? If you didn't know Dalton, it
doesn't matter. If you did, I am merely asking
you to tell me about the coin."

Hoskins narrowed his eyes, then dropped his
hands to clasp the armrests of his chair. "You
know what, young man? I like you."

This guy was just full of surprises. Frankie
nodded. He could feel a *"but"* coming.

"Yep. You remind me of my little brother,
Johnny. He was the youngest of four kids, just
as you are."

"The internet mentioned that, too?"

"Isn't that thing great? But my point is Johnny
started out a little rough around the edges just
as you did, and now he's a tenured professor at

Berkeley. Sometimes the youngest in a household of boys has to work hard to stand out. Sometimes, the way they stand out becomes... problematic. But he turned himself around and I believe you have, as well."

Frankie, damn near speechless, mumbled his thanks. What the heck?

"Come with me," Hoskins added.

He sprang to his feet and walked nimbly across the room to unlock and throw open the small door Frankie had noticed upon arriving.

They entered an unexpectedly opulent office with plush carpets, rich wood furniture, beautiful paintings, sleek computers and even a floor-to-ceiling antique wooden wine rack set into a far wall. Hoskins walked past the desk to the wine rack. Frankie expected the older man to pop out a bottle for them to celebrate... well, what? The fact that Johnny Hoskins had straightened out his life?

Instead, Hoskins dug in his pocket and withdrew a medallion shaped like a bunch of grapes with a couple of leaves. It matched an embossed decoration on the shelves. He inserted the ornament in the bookcase, pushed it with one finger and the whole unit pivoted on its axis.

Hoskins repocketed the medallion, reached inside and flipped on a light illuminating a flight of descending stairs. "Come along," he called to Frankie who sidled past him into the steep stairwell. When he glanced over his shoulder, he saw that Hoskins had silently closed the wine rack/door behind them and followed.

The stairs led to a cellar now ablaze with lights. There were no windows, nothing to advertise its existence aboveground. The brick walls were lined with charts, degrees, framed newspaper articles, some yellowed and old. What looked like a digital magnifier occupied a table while box upon box of presentation cases had been inserted into slots built into shelves made specifically for this purpose. All appeared to be carefully labeled.

"Of course I knew Dave," Hoskins said, sitting in a swivel chair behind a pile of other equipment including ultraviolet lamps, mint sheet albums and a coin scale. He motioned for Frankie to take a seat. "I can't help you when it comes to his death except to say the man seemed very content and happy. But one never knows. Money can't buy peace."

His words, spoken in one context, struck Frankie in another. He was banking on the fact Jay Thurman could be bought off, but for how long? It wasn't a permanent fix. What was? Maybe a nice big truck running over the oaf? Hey, a man could dream.

"This is quite a setup," Frankie commented.

"It's the heart of my business," Hoskins said. "The Boise address is my public face." He steepled his fingers again and peered at Frankie. "I knew Dave had a bunch of these coins and I was only too happy to get my hands on them," he finally said. "He kept his fortune private out of concern about theft, but mostly because he couldn't explain where he got them or how, and didn't want the government getting involved and demanding their share. That's about the extent of what he confided to me. I, too, am cautious or have been until now. You know the truth about me. What you choose to do with it I suppose is up to you."

"I'm not interested in trying to solve the mystery of Dalton's coins unless they somehow tie in to the robbery and I just don't see how they do. Will you tell me about the coins now?"

"I'll do better than that," Hoskins said and, taking a key from around his neck, unlocked a file drawer from which he withdrew a ring of keys. He selected one of these and inserted it in his desk drawer. A second later, he produced a small display case that held a single gold coin.

"This is the only one I have left," Hoskins said. "It's a 1904 Liberty, US Mint Gold Double Eagle, worth twenty dollars at the time. This one is uncirculated although some of his coins showed modest signs of wear."

"What did you pay for it?"

"I gave him fifteen hundred for this one. I have a buyer interested for twice that. And as you know, the coins stolen from the Green Ridge Bank were exactly this mint."

"Did he ever give any indication how many there were?"

"Dave could be cagey. I might not have been the only one he dealt with. I got the feeling there were a lot of coins, maybe hundreds. If they did come from the Green Ridge bank robbery, they must have been hidden away. It seems unlikely there would be any left if they'd been dipped into over all the intervening years—to me, it seems they must have been recovered within the last few years."

"One more thing," Frankie said. "Did Dalton ever mention the existence of a letter that came along with the coins?"

"A letter? No, not a word. What kind of letter?"

"I don't think anyone knows," Frankie said.

Hoskins handed the small display case to Frankie who studied the tiny embossed stars encircling Lady Liberty's head. The coin didn't answer any questions; in fact, it posed others. He handed the display case back to Hoskins and thanked him.

Hoskins locked the coin back in his drawer.

Ten minutes later, Frankie was back in his truck where he placed a call to Sara.

"I don't think Ed Hoskins had a thing to do with your dad's death," he said once she'd answered. "He admits he bought the coins. As I was leaving, he made a point of telling me to tell you that he would be delighted to discuss buying any you'd care to liquidate."

"Is he a trustworthy guy?"

"Within reason," Frankie said thinking neither Sara nor Hoskins were going to win any awards for honesty when it came to the disposition of those coins.

As soon as he hit the open highway, his thoughts leaped past the impending visit with his mother to the ten o'clock appointment with Jay Thurman.

KATE WAS BACK on the bench in front of the river when Frankie drove into the area between the house and barn. She couldn't deny her heart lifted at the sight of his truck and she got to her feet, wincing as her knee throbbed. She'd taken a tumble late in the afternoon as she attempted to climb a promising rock in her seemingly endless search.

Between the unsuccessful morning riverside excursion and the two later in the day—to say nothing of the ride to the ghost town—it had been a full day. Back in Seattle, she spent her time tending her grandmother and trying to fix up the house. Those chores took physical as well as mental strength, but the muscles engaged were not the ones required to walk and climb and descend rocky cliffs or ride horses. The end result was that she was acquiring a broadening collection of aches and pains.

And that didn't even begin to address the newest wrinkle: worry about Frankie. She didn't know what he was hiding but it sounded serious. Jay Thurman was dangerous, hence, Frankie was in trouble. It didn't sound as though he was going to allow anyone to watch his back and that scared her.

She needed to wangle an invitation to go with him.

Frankie smiled and paused when he noticed Kate coming toward him and some of the awkwardness with which they'd parted earlier dissipated. "Are you limping?" he asked, eyebrows furled.

"Just a little. Did you learn anything from Mr. Hoskins?"

"Yes and no," he said, peering down at her face. His gray eyes were as beautiful as ever, but she could see worry lurking in their depths. "Hoskins bought Dalton's coins," Frankie continued. "He even showed me one. Beautiful thing. He said most he saw were uncirculated. That fits in with what we know of the payroll shipment that was stolen. But as for any leads on Dalton's death—he doesn't know any more than you and I do. I think if Sara is convinced her father was murdered she's going to have to tell the police and chance losing the treasure. They can't investigate if they don't have a reason to suspect anything."

"But she promised her father," Kate said softly.

"A promise to a dead man? Does that take precedence over everything else?"

And that was a good—if uncomfortable—question. Kate had no intention of thinking about it right now, however, let alone trying to answer.

"What did you do this afternoon?" he asked. He glanced down at the tear in her jeans and then back at her face, using a finger to gently turn her head so her cheek was toward him. "You have scratches. Are you okay?"

"I fell."

"By the river?"

"Yes, as a matter of fact, by the river."

"Are you sure you're all right? Grace used to be a nurse."

"I don't need a nurse," she said breezily. "Besides, Grace and your dad are back at the hospital with Gerard and Kinsey. She's in labor again."

"Man, I hope it works out this time. All these stops and starts make me nervous," Frankie said.

She touched his hand. "What are you doing later? Could we get together?"

"Mom should be here any minute. I'd better figure out something for dinner."

He'd completely ignored her question. "I forgot to tell you that Grace left some kind of chicken dish in the slow cooker."

"That was nice of her," he said, but his attention had been drawn to a car now crossing the bridge. "That'll be my mother," he said, and they walked to the parking area, arriving about the same time as the car. The driver turned out to be a wispy blonde wearing jeans and a white shirt. As soon as she got out of the car, she took Frankie's hands and beamed up at him.

Kate stared at her in a little bit of disbelief. It was obvious she was Frankie's mother but at first glance, she appeared more like his sister. They shared the same gray eyes and high cheekbones. Features that looked masculine on him somehow looked ultra-feminine on her.

After a brief hug, she stretched her arms above her head. "I am so stiff from driving. I can't believe I have to turn around and leave in an hour."

"Just an hour?" Frankie said.

"Yes. I'm meeting a friend in Boise at ten o'clock for a séance."

Ten o'clock. The time hung there for a second and then Frankie spoke. "Mom, this is Kate," he said. "Kate, my mother, Vivian."

"How nice to meet you," Vivian said, shaking Kate's hand. Vivian had to be close to fifty, but time had treated her well. Her skin showed no trace of makeup and was relatively unlined.

"Frankie, dear, what's wrong?" Vivian said as she studied him.

"Nothing," Frankie said uneasily.

"Your shoulders are full of tension," she said. "And your eyes…"

"It's been a long day, that's all," Frankie said, glancing down at Kate. How many times since she'd arrived on this ranch had she found herself in his exact position, caught between an unspoken truth and a reluctant lie of omission? Part of her knew she should be relieved it was him under scrutiny instead of her, but all she felt was sorry that she couldn't share his burden.

Vivian looked unconvinced. "I met a mystic in India this winter. He guided me on a spiritual journey inside my subconscious. I'm very sensitive to everything now, especially my one and only son."

"Let's go inside and have a bite to eat," he said.

"Oh, no, no thank you," she said. "I've gone vegan and I try to never impose my eating preferences on others. That's why I had a fruit smoothie in Falls Bluff. You two go ahead…"

Both Frankie and Kate said the same thing at the same moment. "I'm not really hungry," they broke off and smiled at each other.

"I only have a little while and there's something I want to talk to you about."

"I should leave you two alone," Kate mumbled.

"That isn't necessary," Vivian said with a smile. "I'm sure Frankie won't want to keep things from his girlfriend."

Both Frankie and Kate jumped in with denials that Vivian more or less ignored. "Is the old arbor still standing?" she asked.

"Yeah," Frankie said. "Let's go sit down." He led them to the front of the house to an area Kate hadn't noticed as it was shielded by the house itself and a lot of trees. The patio sported a brick floor and a wrought-iron table and chairs covered with a slatted roof. It reminded Kate at once of Frankie's tree house. A wall of climbing roses perfumed the evening air.

"I've always loved this spot," Vivian said as she took a chair and looked around. "It hasn't changed much in thirty years, has it? The roses are a nice touch, though."

As soon as the others were seated, she leaned forward. "Frankie, dear, do you remember how you were always asking me about my side of the family?"

"Yes, of course I do," he said. "You never had much to tell me."

"I know. My mother didn't talk much."

"Then you don't remember any more?"

"We'll get to that. First of all, I heard from a man who says he works with you and someone named Gary."

"Gary Dodge. Yeah, he's the producer of the documentary I wrote you about. Who contacted you?"

"He said his name was Pat."

"Pat Lowell," Frankie said.

"That's right. He said he's doing some background type work."

"Yeah, on the old ghost town."

"Well, he told me that he's uncovered proof that my grandmother lived in Green Ridge until 1915 when she moved away."

"The year the town started to die," Frankie said. "Wait a second… Dad told me you were looking for someone back when you guys met.

Did you suspect you might be related to some-one from the ghost town?"

"Yes. Well, kind of. My great-aunt had men-tioned my grandmother just once or twice. Her name was Mamie. I was told she'd lived in Green Ridge way back when and at first I thought I'd see if I could find out anything about her. Great Aunt said Mamie was a hellion of sorts, a real spitfire in her youth. The fact she had spirit attracted me.

"But she's not the main reason I came here. See, my father came from around these parts, too. He was a…troubled…man. I knew he had another family before he married my mother and I wanted to find them and see if he'd done to his first daughter what he did to me."

She swallowed hard. "My father was an ac-countant for the county, but he was also a sex-ual predator. When I finally got up the nerve to tell my mother about his middle-of-the-night visits to my room, she called me a liar and kicked me out of the house. Keep in mind I was thirteen years old. I went to live with my father's elderly aunt who told me about his first family, a wife and a daughter, who lived out-side Falls Bluff, Idaho. She hadn't heard from them in years but I knew that meant I had an older sister and I started wondering what she was…like."

"Did you ever find her?" Kate asked.

"She and her mother died in a house fire about two weeks before I got here. My estranged parents are dead now, too. Everyone's gone." She glanced at Frankie and added, "I never told Harry about any of this. What was the point? And once he and I got engaged, I stopped thinking about Mamie and the past. I put it all behind me." Vivian had grown somber during this difficult conversation and now turned her palms upward, closed her eyes, took a deep cleansing breath and exhaled.

"The past is the past," she whispered like a chant. "The future is what's important." She patted the back of Frankie's hand. "However, I know you're curious. My father's past is a dead end now, but maybe you can find out something about Mamie."

"No last name?"

"None that I know of. I don't know what happened to her."

Frankie was quiet for a moment. "Mamie can be a nickname for Mary," he finally said. "A woman named Mary Dalton left with her husband and his son soon after the robbery. Dalton seems to have been a semi-invalid but it's possible he's connected to the stolen coins." He studied his mother's face for a second. "You might be related to Mary Dalton, Mom. That would mean I am, too."

She glanced at her watch and stood up. "Okay, I've done what I came to do, I've told you things you always wanted to know. Forgive me, but I have to go. I'll be back in the States around Christmas." She narrowed her eyes as she studied him and then added, "I still sense something is bothering you. My advice is to search inward. Nice to meet you, Kate."

They moved around to the parking area again and Vivian hugged her son one last time before driving away with a wave.

"She's pretty amazing," Kate said in her wake.

Frankie put his arm around her shoulders. "I had no idea her father had done that to her," he said. "I always wished I could have met him—now I'm glad I never did."

"I don't blame you."

"No wonder she's been running away from her past her whole life. I'm kind of glad to understand that it—"

"That it what?" she promoted when he paused.

"That it wasn't me she was running from," he finally said. He watched the dust trail for a few moments, then looked back at Kate. "But you know what I keep wondering? Why did Pat

contact her about this link to her great-grand-
mother instead of me?"

"Odd, isn't it?" Kate said.

"Very."

Chapter Fourteen

Frankie drove up to The Three Aces and parked off to the side. The clock on his dashboard showed he was thirty minutes early but that's what he wanted. It was risky to let Jay call all the shots. The guy was the give-me-an-inch-and-I'll-take-a-mile type.

For a second he paused and looked down the steep slope to the tiny ribbon of the Bowline River flowing below. Forevermore he would think of it as Kate's river and long after she'd disappeared from his life, her beautiful face would come back to haunt him whenever he glimpsed its shores. As the river ran through the ranch, that promised to happen several times a day.

It had been a little awkward between them after his mother left, as though both of them were waiting for something to happen. Well, that's exactly what he was doing—waiting to come here, to hear Jay out. He had no idea what had been on her mind only that he'd found himself evading her suggestions they take a drive or go for a walk. The intimacy he'd struggled to create now worked against him. He wanted to tell her what was going on but didn't dare. His only hope was that he could buy off Jay for a little while so he could establish more of a relationship with Kate. Then when the time came to tell her the truth about himself, she'd know him well enough to see that he'd changed. He also needed time to figure out how to reveal to his dad the lies he'd told to get himself out of trouble.

An hour before he had to leave, Kate had finally given up and said good-night. With tremendous regret, he watched her walk down the hall to her bedroom, knowing he'd hurt her feelings but was powerless to fix it. In a super funk, he'd driven back to the tree house to get ready for this meeting but for the first time, the frivolous nature of the structure seemed to mock him. A tree house demanded a light heart.

As he passed by the usual crowd at the bar, he recognized Pete Richards, the kid who had worked summers on the ranch during high school. They greeted each other but Frankie kept moving. He was on edge about the coming meeting and wanted to find an out-of-the-way table.

After choosing a relatively dark corner with a clear view of the door, he ordered ice tea served in a whiskey glass, hold the ice. No need to advertise the fact he wasn't drinking. He glanced around to see if he knew anyone else. Neighbors a mile or two up the road were celebrating something at one table, a couple of the guys who worked at the hardware store in Falls Bluff sat talking over cold beers. No one else stood out though many sat with their backs to him and he wondered if Jay was biding his time among them.

That question was answered when the front door opened and Jay stepped into the room. A sort of hush descended, then some of their mutual cronies greeted him. He punched a couple on the arm, but he'd obviously seen Frankie sitting in the back and without hesitation made his way to the table, a cigarette dangling from his thick lips.

"So, you came," he said with a smug smile. He ground out the cigarette and sat down heavily in his chair. He needed a shave and a change of clothes. Stale cigarette smoke clung to him like dust mites.

"How much is it going to cost me to keep you quiet?" Frankie said, in no mood for small talk.

Jay sat down and signaled the waitress. "Double whiskey," he ordered and waited until she walked out of earshot. "It's going to cost you gold," he said.

"I don't have gold," Frankie said, but his heart kind of dropped. Why would he ask for gold? "Give me a cash number and I'll see what I can do."

"I heard via the grapevine that the old bank robbery loot is on your land and that you're figuring on digging it up for a movie."

Frankie shook his head. "Where did you hear a tall tale like that?"

"Around. People talk."

"Well, someone is pulling your leg," Frankie said, leaning back in his chair in an effort to strike a relaxed, unthreatened pose. As he did this, he caught sight of Pete Richards turning to stare at their table. Pete had overheard his family discussing the gold coins. He must have told Jay. That had to be it. The younger man turned quickly away and Frankie bit back a groan.

"Remember that guy on TV who opened Al Capone's vault?" Jay said. "All the cameras were rolling and the thing was empty." Laughter shot from his mouth. "Man, can you imagine how humiliating that must have been?"

"That was a live show," Frankie said as Jay lit up another cigarette. "Even if we could figure out where to look for the 'loot', we wouldn't be in that position. But you've got your facts—"

"Don't even try it," Jay said, eyes narrowing. "I know you're lying." He sat up straight and smiled as the server delivered his drink. He spoke a couple of lewd comments to her that Frankie suddenly realized were attempts at flirting. The woman rolled her eyes and left. Jay turned his attention back to Frankie. "You've got twenty-four hours to tell me where it is."

"I can't because I don't know. And even if I did, I wouldn't. The gold doesn't belong to either one of us."

"You're talking pretty tough for a guy with so much to lose."

"It's all immaterial," Frankie insisted, "because I don't even have a hint where it is."

"Says you. Stop stalling. We'll get to it first and take what we want. When the others go after it, they'll just think it was restolen years before. No one will know we took it now."

"I'll know," Frankie said, his jaw clenched.

"And you'll live with it." He took the cigarette from his lips and tossed back the drink. "This is serious money and I intend to have it. Help me and we share. Stand in my way and you'll lose a whole lot more than your family's respect."

"What are you talking about?" Frankie demanded.

"That cute little blonde, for instance…"

HE DROVE AROUND after leaving the bar. He'd done the same thing night after night when he was a late teen when he'd been too restless to stay inside the house. Since his father didn't approve of this behavior, he'd had to climb out on the roof and jump down to the top of the arbor, then leap to the ground, ride a bike to the hay barn and "borrow" the truck. Getting back inside was trickier. The year his dad installed a trellis for the roses fixed that problem, though.

He was restless again.

There was no running from the current impossible situation but the fact could not be ignored that he didn't know where the gold was or if it was still around and even if he did, he wasn't about to tell Jay of all people, let alone be part of stealing it. There was nothing to do but come clean and tell his father the truth. Not tonight—it was too late to wade into all that tonight. Tomorrow morning would have to do.

Back home, he cast a regretful look toward the ranch house and detoured onto his own little road. The drive to his tree house that usually filled him with anticipation and contentment did neither tonight. He parked close to the tree, got out of the truck and stopped dead when he heard a noise approaching him from the dark. He fumbled in his pocket for the remote that controlled the lights and clicked them on, thinking he was going to start carrying a sidearm until this was over.

Kate stood holding Ginger's reins. She blinked at the light, then covered her mouth with her hands as her eyes grew huge. Dropping the reins, she ran to Frankie who caught her.

"What's wrong?" he asked as she trembled in his arms. "Are you okay?" He leaned back to study her face. "Did someone hurt you?" Had Jay come here?

"Where have you been?" she cried, gazing up at him and he was alarmed to see fear on her face.

"Driving around," he said. "Kate, what's wrong?"

For several seconds she couldn't seem to answer and his head raced through scenarios, each one more terrible than the one before. He looked her over from head to toe. "Kate, talk to me. What happened?"

"Nothing!" she finally blurted. "I thought… I thought something happened to you. I didn't know if I should ask for help or…" She gripped his arms and looked up at him. "Oh, Frankie, Frankie…"

He pulled her close and claimed her lips. The urgent rush of need that flooded his body coupled with the shock of finding her here and in this state made his head reel. He kissed her until they were both limp, then he stared into her eyes. "Come upstairs," he whispered.

"Yes."

"Hang on a second," he added and quickly slipped off Ginger's bridle and saddle and laid them on the ground. The horse wandered off. He knew she was safe—this was home territory and she'd find a nice patch of juicy grass to amuse herself before wandering back to the barn.

All this was done in virtual silence. At last he led Kate up the ramp. He'd locked the door before leaving but he still checked the place over before pulling her inside where he immediately folded her in his arms and held her like the very real, warm, soft lifeline she was. The few minutes between kissing her on the ground and kissing her in the boughs of the tree had done nothing to dampen the desire that sparked between them like a high-voltage wire.

Clenched together, they moved toward the bed, shedding clothes along the way. It was relatively dark inside the house as he hadn't opened the blinds—no Peeping Toms tonight, not now, not with her. Instead just the passion-driven energy that guided their hands and bodies. "I can't believe you're here," he whispered at one point and she laughed very softly.

He knew it was crazy, he knew it made no

sense but he also knew that she was the one, there would never be another. He wanted to make everything perfect for her—champagne, roses, music, candles—but that wasn't going to happen, not this first time. This time they would hurl through space, whizzing past stars and planets, two bodies rocketing together... next time would be romance. This time discovery fueled the flames.

There were a million words hovering on his lips, words he wouldn't say, words that weren't needed anyway. She was soft and yet demanding, her passion an equal match for his own, her body ripe and succulent, yielding. Every touch, every kiss, every moan amplified and quadrupled until they reached the peak of ecstasy and fell back to earth—together...

For a second or two he rested his weight on her. When he kissed her lips, he found them salty.

"Are you crying?" he whispered.

"No," she said, but obviously she was.

"Did I hurt you?"

She shook her head and he moved aside, propping his head on his hand to look down at her face. With his free hand, he touched her cheek and she closed her hand around his.

"Nothing's wrong," she said softly.

"But the tears—"

"—are ones of relief, of happiness, that's all," she said.

He leaned over and kissed her lips again. "You look beautiful," he said. "Like an angel."

She smiled. "So do you. Oh, Frankie, don't ever scare me like that again."

"I'll try not to," he said softly, his fingers grazing her petal-soft skin. His heart was as full as it had ever been, practically bursting. "You're incredible," he whispered into her hair. "You're perfect."

"No," she protested.

He lowered his head to kiss the succulent nipple of each breast. "Yes, you are," he said.

"Oh, those things," she said dismissively. "They just seem to get bigger and bigger."

"I'm not complaining," he said, inching his way up to kiss her lips again.

For a while they just lay in each other's arms, too comfortable to think about moving. But Frankie kept seeing her face when he drove into the clearing. "Why were you in such a panic?" he whispered at last.

She didn't respond immediately. He drew back and waited. She finally swallowed. "Frankie, I know where you went tonight," she muttered.

Her words could not have shocked him more than if she'd announced she was an alien. All the cozy, hopeful thoughts that had chased fear and worry away a second before now trembled in a corner. He sat up abruptly. "What do you know?" he asked looking back down at her.

She, too, sat. With one hand, she smoothed her hair behind her ear, with the other, she held the comforter against her breasts. "I know about Jay," she said.

"Oh, no," he groaned. "How in the world—"

"I came back last night after you took me home. I missed you and…well, you weren't here but someone else was. Before I could figure out how to sneak away without him hearing me, you showed up and by then I was curious and a little nervous for some reason."

"For good reason," he said softly.

"Frankie, I know he threatened you. I've wanted to ask if you'd need my help all day but it's been…awkward."

"I know," he admitted.

"I just never found the courage. I thought I would at least go up to The Three Aces and be there in case he caused trouble, but everyone around here is gone and I couldn't just take a car. When you didn't come home, I became so worried. I wondered if I should try to find one of your brothers and get them to go look for you. I didn't know if that would just make things worse so I rode back here one last time to see if you'd come home without my knowing, and when I was about to give up, you arrived. Only I didn't know at first it was you. I was just so relieved you were okay."

He leaned his head against hers for a moment. "You heard Jay tell me I had a Get Out of Jail Free card because of my father, didn't you?"

"Yes, I did hear that. But he doesn't strike me as the kind of man to see things as they really are."

"You're right about him, but what he said about my dad was the truth. I should have gone to jail. I would have gone to jail if Dad hadn't moved heaven and earth to get me the best lawyer in Idaho. And he did that because I swore I didn't know what Jay was capable of, that I'd had no part in the violence. Some of that was true, but some wasn't. I've been living with my duplicity ever since."

"So, what happened ten years ago was serious enough for involvement with the law," she said.

"Yes." He considered letting the details drop, but it was crunch time. He'd just made love to her and it hadn't been casual and it hadn't been…unimportant. "You might as well hear it from me. Jay is a few years older than I am. At the time, I was still a minor but he wasn't. One night we drank a few beers and planned a robbery. Not like a bank or anything, just a convenience store a few miles outside town. It was more like playing a fantasy game than plotting reality. By the next morning, we'd sobered up and laughed the idea off. That was it until three days later when Jay showed up at the ranch. He said he was restless and wanted to go for a drive but his car was giving him trouble. I offered to drive and off we went. After a while, he told me to pull in to the store we were passing because he wanted to buy cigarettes. It wasn't until I'd stopped the truck that I realized where we were—the same place we'd talked about a few nights before. He said he'd be back in a minute and disappeared inside.

"Fast forward a few minutes. All of a sudden, I hear a gunshot and a woman scream. Next thing I know, Jay is running out of the store. Laughing like a maniac, he dived into the passenger seat and told me to get the hell out of there. I glanced in the rearview mirror as I started the truck. Two people came running out of the store. I panicked. We tore out of there like nobody's business.

"I found out later he took fifty dollars out of the cash register. The store owner ended up with a bullet in his head for fifty lousy bucks. The guy didn't die but he was in the hospital for months. When he got out, he sold his store and moved away."

"But you didn't know Jay had a gun, did you?"

"No! Still, I knew he was a loose cannon. I let him go alone into a store we'd joked about robbing. Worse, I drove him away from the scene of the crime instead of running inside to do what I could to help because, face it, I was terrified. He was waving that gun around. He wanted to go hit another store…"

"What did you do?"

"I ditched him and thought about running away…eventually I did the one bright thing I'd done since meeting him and that's turn myself in to the sheriff's department."

"That showed responsibility," she said.

"Well, better late than never maybe, but before you start thinking I had shaped up, let me finish. I told my father I was completely innocent, that I hadn't known what Jay had planned, that he'd merely said he was going to buy cigarettes, that he'd forced me to drive away. Jay disagreed with this version of the story, of course, but he was a perpetual liar with a record and a history of violence and I was a screwed-up rich kid that every parent hopes they don't get but kind of understands if they do. The fact I had never really hurt anyone was my saving grace. But Kate, man, I didn't want you to know what I'd done until you knew me better, until you trusted me."

She cupped his cheeks and touched his lips

with hers. "I do trust you, Frankie. That's why I'm here."

He buried his face in the crook of her neck. How could she offer him such acceptance on the cusp of hearing what he'd done? The fact that she did warmed his heart more than he could say and he knew he would work to make sure he never disappointed her or hurt her.

But a nagging feeling tugged at him—Jay's last threat about the pretty blonde. Was Kate safe here? What if Jay targeted her to get to him?

He would not let that happen.

"I spent my college years doing community service," he added because it was important she know he tried to repair what he'd done. "And I worked my butt off for a lot longer than that to pay retribution to the store owner. I apologized to him, but why should he have given a damn? Nothing that happened to me compared to Jay's ten years of hard time."

She looked deep into his eyes. "Try to remember your crimes were different in magnitude."

He nestled his face in the crook of her neck. "Have you ever in your life done anything that shamed you down to the essence of your soul?" he whispered but she didn't answer. There was a chance she hadn't heard him but he thought it far more likely she chose not to answer because she didn't want to have to admit that of course she hadn't, that most people never did.

Whatever her reasons, he appreciated her effort but he knew what he'd done and how it had affected people. For now it was enough to put his arms around her, to bury himself in her lovely flesh and for them both to pass what remained of the night in each other's arms.

LONG AFTER FRANKIE'S even breathing announced he'd fallen asleep on his stomach with his arm draped over her abdomen, Kate lay awake listening to the sounds of the night. She heard an owl hooting nearby and the tiny footsteps of squirrels scampering across the roof. As the night wore on, a breeze stirred the boughs. The house didn't exactly rock, but the creaking and rattling sounds of wooden boughs made her feel as though she was aboard a boat anchored in a moorage as opposed to a house anchored in a tree.

She still felt warmed by the afterglow of Frankie's decision to entrust her with information he'd let fester in his heart for years. In a good world, she would now share with him the network of lies and half-truths she'd used to come to this ranch. In an even better world, he would help her figure this out and she would help him with Jay Thurman. But Jay wanted money; that was clear from what he'd said the night she overheard him talking to Frankie. If there was one thing she couldn't offer, that was it.

Frankie made a soft sound in his sleep, startled perhaps by a dream. His arm tightened across her abdomen and he turned his head so that his warm breath bathed her shoulder.

In a perfect world, this night would never end.

Chapter Fifteen

Kate wasn't sure how she would be greeted the next morning when she arrived back at the ranch with Frankie instead of wandering down the hall from her bedroom alone. As they drove up to the ranch, they could see several cars in the drive and Ginger standing outside the corral looking in at the other horses. They took care of her needs first before entering the main house.

"It's a boy!" Grace said the minute they walked into the room. She was drinking coffee at the counter. "You should see him, Frankie. He's just beautiful. I have a new grandson! Charlie will be so excited there's another child on the ranch to play with."

"That's great news," Frankie said.

"How is Kinsey?" Kate asked.

"Tired but beaming."

"Grace," Frankie said, "where's Dad?"

"He got an early morning call from Soda

Springs. They have the one and only existing part to fix that blasted pump."

"You're kidding me," Frankie said.

"I know. It's some little esoteric thingamajig on a machine he's been nursing for years. I told him to get a new one. I normally would have gone for him, but with Kinsey coming home this morning—"

"She's home already?" Kate interrupted.

"Yes. As a matter of fact, she said to send you over as soon as you want to come." She looked back at Frankie. "Is something the matter, honey?"

"No," Frankie said immediately. "But I need to talk to Dad as soon as he gets home. It's important."

"He won't be back until dark," Grace said. "Soda Springs is a long ways away."

Kate wasn't positive what Jay had threatened Frankie with but now she guessed it had to do with spreading the truth about Frankie's participation in that robbery. If Frankie was asking about his father, it might mean he intended to bypass Jay's blackmail. She was nervous for him but also relieved. If he'd given in to whatever demands Jay made, it would be like handing the man a loaded gun to use whenever he wanted.

"How is Gerard?" Frankie asked.

Grace ginned. "On cloud nine."

"Want to go over and see the baby right now?" Frankie asked Kate.

"Maybe we should wait and let them settle in."

"I'll be busy later, but if you want to go alone—"

"They're not sleeping, trust me," Grace said. "Tell Kinsey I'll be up to help her after I finish things here but she can call if she needs me sooner."

"We will," Frankie said.

They decided to walk up the road and Kate was pleased beyond reason that Frankie took hold of her hand. "I didn't ask you last night," she said. "How much does Jay want to keep quiet?"

"A lot."

"More than you have?"

"More than I have. More than I'm willing to give even if I did have it."

"What are you going to do?" she asked. As always, the river drew her attention, the glimmering water taunting her. Somewhere along its bending curves a treasure lay hidden...a treasure that belonged to her grandmother and that her grandmother needed. Had she lost sight of this goal in her elation over finding Frankie? Perhaps, but it was back now in the cold light of day. That didn't mean she didn't have to fight the urge to tell Frankie everything, to ask for advice, maybe even help.

This was weakness on her part, she knew that, but it was something else, too...

"I'm going to tell Dad just like I should have years before."

"That's what I thought. Good for you."

He shook his head. "I have to admit I dread it. It's taken me so long to earn back his respect. It kills me to ruin it, but there isn't another choice."

She stopped walking and he turned around to face her. "Is something wrong?" he asked.

She stepped up close to him and raised her face to his. His lips were cool from the morning air, but there was also an undercurrent of thrilling heat and suddenly she wished they were back at the tree house. "I'm here for you," she said. "I don't know what I can do, but just ask and I'll try."

He smiled as he touched her face. "Thank you. The same goes for me in regards to you, you know that, right? You can tell me anything. But the only thing I want you to do concerning Jay Thurman is stay away from him."

"Okay," she said slowly.

"Which brings me to asking how your grandmother is doing," he added. "I know you called her while I was showering this morning."

"They say she's fine. She can't talk on the phone, you know. It's kind of like she's disappeared inside that building."

"You'll see her soon, I promise," he said, and kissed her forehead. "Let's go meet the newest Hastings."

Kate was startled by the inside of Kinsey and Gerard's house. Paintings adorned every wall and most of them used the Hastings Ridge Ranch and its inhabitants, both human and otherwise, as models. Everyone Kate had met was shown doing something or caught in a portrait. She'd heard about Kinsey's artistic talent, of course, and even seen examples of it in Frankie's place and around the ranch house, but she was stunned by the detail and quality, to say nothing of the sheer volume that resided in this two-story house.

"What did you name your baby?" she asked Gerard after Frankie introduced him. He was older than Frankie, very handsome and steady-looking with the bluest eyes she'd ever seen.

"Andrew," he said and for the first time she knew what people meant when they said a voice could caress a name.

"Is it a family name?"

"No, although his middle one is Harrison, like my father."

"Andrew Harrison Hastings," Frankie said. "That's a good name. May we see him?"

"Of course. Come on, I'll take you upstairs."

He ushered them into a pretty bedroom filled with baby stuff. But what drew Kate's attention was the woman propped up by pillows in a large overstuffed rocking chair, a bundle of yellow blankets cradled in her arms. Kinsey's smile was a tad on the weary side, but you could tell it came straight from the heart. As Frankie and Kate moved closer, she lowered the baby to rest on her knees and pulled aside the blankets.

"Oh, he's precious," Kate gushed. She hadn't been around too many newborns in her life, the last one a good three years before when a fellow teacher gave birth to a baby girl. This little guy had a dark fuzz and slate eyes. He looked round and pretty and so tiny.

"Isn't he huge?" Kinsey said.

Kate wasn't sure how to respond to that remark.

"Eight pounds two ounces," Kinsey added.

"He's perfect," Gerard said. "But when you're as vertically challenged as my beautiful wife, that's a lot of baby."

They all chuckled and stood around admiring tiny fingers and itsy-bitsy toes until Gerard and Frankie went off to discuss ranch business and Kinsey and Kate were left alone.

"Do you want to hold him?" Kinsey asked.

"Okay," Kate said and sat down on the ottoman beside the rocker. With utmost tenderness, Kinsey transferred her baby to Kate.

"You're a natural," Kinsey said as she looked at Kate cuddling her son. "Look, he's staring at you."

It did seem the little guy was peering upward at Kate who smiled back. His features were so small and sweet, his little mouth like a rosebud. "He's wonderful," she said. "He smells so good."

"I wanted you to have a chance to see what it's like. I know when I was pregnant and a lady in town let me hold her newborn it made it real for me in a way it hadn't been until then. When is yours due?"

Kate's brow wrinkled. "My what?"

"Your baby."

"My what?" she repeated so sharply it startled the baby in her arms. She instantly rocked him and apologized to Kinsey. "I'm so sorry, I didn't mean to scare him."

"It's okay."

"You better take him back," Kate said.

Kinsey took her son and held him up against

her chest. The baby fussed for thirty seconds, then appeared to fall asleep.

"I'm not pregnant," Kate said, staring at Kinsey.

"I thought—"

"Why would you think such a thing?"

"Well, you were saying that for the last two months you've been dizzy and weepy and tired and nauseated…it sounded exactly like my first trimester. Plus my breasts did just what yours have done. And there's a kind of, oh, a look about you, a kind of inner glow—oh, God, I am so sorry. Listen to me rambling. Can you forgive me?"

Kate heard every word Kinsey said but even as she listened, her mind raced backward in time. When had she last slept with Luke? Not for a long time…

But no, that wasn't true. She knew she'd tried to erase the fact it had happened from her mind but one night three or four months ago, she'd let her guard down and slept with him. When she found out the next day that he'd left for Alaska, she'd been mortified. Had he assumed they were back together, was that what had propelled him into making the decision to risk his life?

"Kate, are you all right?"

Kate swallowed a lump of air and nodded.

"Blink," Kinsey said.

She blinked.

"Take a deep breath," Kinsey added. "Go on."

Kinsey took a deep breath. She finally met Kinsey's gaze.

"You look like you've seen a ghost," Kinsey whispered.

Kate licked her lips. "In a way, I have."

FRANKIE LEFT KATE at the house. He knew darn well that she would be back at the river before he got as far as the field where they were mowing that day. It was always right on the tip of his tongue to coax an explanation out of her and then he would hear Pat Lowell's voice urging Frankie to give her a chance, she'd been overwhelmed for months, she'd taken science classes… None of that explained what she was doing poking around the Bowline, but he let it pass anyway because he agreed with everything Pat said.

But it went deeper than that. He didn't want to challenge her. He didn't want her to think he thought she was up to no good when she'd been over-the-top understanding of him. And now there was an additional reason: Jay. She was vulnerable as long as she was here and the primary goal had to be to get her away. Maybe on the ride home tomorrow she would be forthright about things.

He'd almost forgotten the original reason she had come to the ranch—the documentary. How could he have forgotten that? And why did it seem she had, as well? He let all this go as he caught up with Chance and Pike both running combines out in the middle of a sun-blazed field. Chance was the closest and Frankie drove his truck over the rutted, mowed field to reach him. Off in the distance, he saw the second combine head their direction.

While they waited for Pike to arrive, Chance produced a cooler and poured glasses of cold water.

Pike's machine finally came to a halt, casting the field into silence. "Hey, Frankie, where have you been?" he asked, wiping the sweat from his brow as he accepted a cold glass from Chance.

"We went to see Gerard's new son," Frankie responded. "Have you seen him yet?"

"No. Lily went over first thing," Chance said, "but I was with Dad out in the equipment barn until he left for Soda Springs. You heard about the part?"

"Yeah. He should have replaced the pump this winter. It's not like everyone didn't warn him," Frankie said.

"What'd they name the baby?" Pike asked.

"Andrew Harrison."

"Big name for the little guy," Chance said. "Did Kate go see him with you?"

"She did." He thought for a moment and added, "She was kind of quiet when we left. I'm not sure—maybe a baby seems so far away for her it kind of makes her sad."

Chance chuckled. "I heard you were suspicious of her."

"Who told you that?"

Pike wiggled an embarrassed finger. "Gerard might have mentioned it," he said.

"I'm getting to know her," Frankie said. "She's hard not to like."

"I hate to change the subject," Pike said, "but I talked to Pete Richards this morning when he came by to pick up his paycheck. He mentioned he saw you at The Three Aces last night with Jay Thurman."

Frankie returned his brother's level-eyed appraisal. "Jay got out of jail a week or so ago." Sometimes being the youngest brother sucked... they all thought they had to police him.

"That guy is trouble," Chance said. "I told you that ten years ago and I'll bet my bottom dollar prison didn't improve him."

"You'd be safe making that bet," Frankie admitted. "He's still the same old Jay."

"You don't owe him anything," Pike said.

"I know that."

"He's the kind to think you do. Frankie—"

"Listen, I'll take care of this myself," Frankie said, anger warming his face.

"I just don't want you—"

"To get in trouble again, to shame the family. I know, I got it, I don't want that, either."

"What I was going to say," Pike said carefully, "is that I just don't want you to think you have to deal with this guy alone. We're brothers. One of us gets punched, we all get punched."

"Oh," he said, suddenly contrite.

"Pete said you looked angry but he also said you looked a little worried. What we're tiptoeing around saying, Frankie, is that Pete got the feeling there was a problem."

"Pete Richards probably helped create it," Frankie said. "Him and his big mouth."

"What does that mean?"

"He told Jay Thurman about the gold supposedly being on our land."

"He did not."

"He had to. How else would Jay have known about it?"

"I don't know, but if Pete told Jay anything I'd eat my hat. You're forgetting about his sister."

"Pete's sister? Paty at the feed store?"

"No, his older one. Kara."

Kara. Frankie thought hard for a second before he conjured up a pretty girl a year or two ahead of him in school.

"Don't you know what he did to her?" Chance said.

"No."

"It was right before you and he...well, before the convenience store thing. He slipped something into Kara's soda and forced himself on her. She refused to press charges so he got away with it. Pete knew about it—he's the one who told us. In other words, Pete hates Jay with a passion."

"I didn't know," Frankie said, his mind racing. It seemed impossible Jay hadn't bragged about a sick act like that. Why hadn't he? Frankie hoped it was because he'd sense Frankie would have drawn the line at such barbarous behavior. The bigger question was this: If Pete didn't say anything about the gold, who did? The answer was impossible to know. He might have told someone who told someone else.

"Maybe you'd better tell us why Jay is talking about gold all of a sudden," Pike said.

Frankie took a deep breath. "I can handle it," he said.

"Frankie, listen to me," Chance pleaded, his eyes intense. "For almost ten years you've been the Hastingses' version of a lone wolf, so tied up in knots about what choices you made that you wouldn't let anyone get too close. Let it go, man. Talk to us."

"He's right," Pike said quietly.

Frankie started to dismiss them, then looked each in the eye.

"Okay," he said, nodding his head.

He paused, uncertain how to start. "Jay seems to know about the possibility of the gold being on this land and he figures I'm a conniving rat like he is so I'll be willing to steal it out from under my family and the documentary and whoever legally owns it to split with him. That's why I thought Pete must have told him about Gary's visit."

"Man, if he didn't, who did?" Chance said.

"Exactly."

"What did you tell him?"

"I told him I didn't know where it was but that even if I did, what he wanted was out of the question."

"So that's the end of it," Pike said.

Frankie shook his head. "I wish. Unfortunately, there's more. He has something he thinks he can hold over my head."

Pike's jaw tightened. "He's blackmailing you?"

"He's trying to. When I didn't back down, he made veiled threats about Kate. He's…seen… us together and he knows I like her."

"So what happens next?" Pike asked.

"By ten o'clock tonight, I'm supposed to have examined my options and decided everyone's feelings about me are more important than things like honesty and honor. He said he'd contact me. He expects me to take him to the gold stash. He simply will not accept that I have no idea where it is or even if it exists. He seems positive it's here and I know about it."

"Brother," Pike said.

"I know."

"What's he using as leverage?" Pike asked.

Frankie met his gaze. "A truth I've kept from Dad. I'll tell you about it after I have an opportunity to talk to him."

Chance laughed, which earned him Pike's and Frankie's attention. "And what's so funny?" Pike asked.

"Us," Chance said. "Remember the old days? Especially me and you, Frankie. Nothing got in our way."

"Well, that throw-caution-to-the-wind attitude didn't work out so hot for me," Frankie said.

"Maybe not, but it made you who you are today. You can only live your own life journey, you know. Few people get close to their thirtieth birthday without making a few mistakes along the way."

Frankie narrowed his eyes, unsure where

Chance was taking all this. Sure, both he and Chance had seldom walked away from confrontation, but Frankie had taken it further than that when he'd broken the law. And Chance? He was one of those guys who had flitted from one woman to the next—until he met Lily and then the world, for him, changed.

"But that's not what I was thinking," Chance added as Frankie stared at him. "I was thinking that Jay has opened himself wide up. In the old days we would have messed with him, all stops ahead, damn the torpedoes."

"What the heck are you talking about?" Pike asked.

"I'm talking about coming up with a plan to make him think he's got this all wrong."

"Oh, brother," Pike said, shaking his head.

Frankie folded his legs and sat down in the freshly mowed grass. "What do you have in mind?" he asked.

Chapter Sixteen

"Remember those old money bags from the Green Ridge Bank?" Chance said as he perched on his haunches. Even Pike had condescended to lean against the combine and listen.

"The ones Dad took when he was a kid?" Frankie asked.

"Yeah. Back when you could still get inside the old bank, before the cave-in. He took a whole stack of them."

"I remember him telling us about that," Frankie said.

"Yeah, he also took the iron grate off the door leading to the vault," Pike said.

"Which is now supporting the climbing rose in the arbor. Anyway, I know where those bags are."

"Where?" Pike asked.

"In the attic above the old cattle barn. They looked like they'd been there for decades and that was fifteen years ago. I came across them when I was showing a young lady the infinite opportunities for privacy on a ranch."

Pike almost smiled. "Really, a loft? Isn't that a cliché even for you?"

"Never underestimate the value of an oldie but goodie. Anyway, Dad must have thrown them there and forgotten about them. They're a little moth-eaten and dirty, but they've got the bank's name printed on them and a big black dollar sign just for the heck of it. Very picturesque, like in an old Western."

"What do we do with the bags?" Pike asked.

"We stage finding them," Chance said, clearly excited, "only to discover they're empty and the real loot is gone, taken a long time ago."

"What do you mean stage finding them?" Frankie persisted.

"Just what I said. We hide them and then lead Jay right to the spot! But the bags are empty, see, and that means the treasure is long gone, stolen again after it was hidden. We could use that cave on Mt. Jinx."

"You mean the old gold mine?"

"No, the cave on the other side of the mountain. We used to play in it when we were kids."

"I remember," Frankie said. "I always thought bears lived in that thing."

"I did, too," Chance said.

They smiled at each other until Pike cleared his throat. "And exactly why would we do all this?" he asked.

Chance opened his mouth as if to explain, and then grinned. "I'm not sure."

Frankie had to laugh. He clapped Chance on the back. "It would be fun, you're right, but don't underestimate Jay Thurman. He can be a real beast when he's thwarted. I'm concerned he's going to take out his aggression on Kate when he finds out I've told Dad the whole sorry truth of the robbery."

"You didn't shoot anyone, did you?" Pike asked.

"No. Of course not."

"Good."

"So, for now I just want to make sure Kate is safe tonight when I go meet Jay."

"She can come to the A-frame with Lily and Charlie," Chance said. "This is Lily's big shopping day and pizza is on the menu."

"You wouldn't mind?"

"Of course not. Then you can take care of business and know she's safe."

"Could she spend the night there? In fact, could both of us?"

"Sure, the place is big." He paused and grinned before adding, "Don't you want her at your tree house?"

Frankie stared from one of them to the other and shook his head. He should have guessed they knew. "You guys know about the tree house?"

Chance nodded. "Pike told me. He found it one day when he was out riding."

"I noticed someone had built a new well by the old one down by the river," Pike explained. "I was curious why anyone would do that."

"Does Dad—"

"I don't think so," Pike said. "I only told Chance when he started worrying about you falling back into old habits. I wanted him to know you were okay."

"Sorry," Chance said.

"No problem," Frankie said. He'd always figured he'd feel kind of trespassed upon if anyone knew what he did on his own time, but to his surprise, no such feeling shadowed his heart. "I guess that's what family does—look out for each other."

"That's right," Pike said as he got to his feet. "That's what family does."

KATE DECIDED TO walk to the river that morning. Not only was it a beautiful day, but she had a whole lot on her mind and liked the feeling of moving one leg in front of the other. However, her pack was heavy and ungainly and she arrived at her destination with a sore back. She forged her way down the steep, eroded, overgrown path that led to the rocky shore, knowing that Frankie's tree house in the forest at her back was probably less than a half a mile away.

For a second, she stared at the rushing water without seeing it. Emotional, weepy, tired, nauseous. Kinsey was right, she'd felt all of these things recently and written them off to worry, grief, guilt—name it, everything had been so easy to explain away.

But a baby? Could it possibly be true? Her free hand drifted toward her abdomen—Gram and a newborn at the same time? How would she take care of two dependent people at such opposite ends of their lives?

If it came to that, she just would. That's all. Somehow, she'd make it work, but now it was hard to ignore the fact that the possibility of finding the diamonds had taken on an added dimension.

A renewed sense of urgency coursed through her veins and it was at that moment that she glimpsed a funny-looking rock on the western end of the beach. It wasn't in the water as the original letter reported, but if you squinted just right and used your imagination, you could almost see a bonnet perched on a head. And from this vantage point, Green Peak, or as Frankie called it, Mt. Jinx, peeked over the tops of the trees on the opposite bank. One hundred years ago the forest between here and there must have been shorter making the mountain look higher.

As she dropped the pack to the ground and continued on for a closer look, she had to marvel at her luck. Was it possible she'd made an eleventh hour discovery? According to the letter, she would need to line up the bonnet with the mountaintop. What about the well foundation, the pile of old rocks she'd been looking for on the other parts of the river? Maybe it had been demolished during the plowing of the road.

No snagged tree, but she hadn't really expected to find that. As she studied the rock, she had the queerest sensation that she'd finally found the spot. Maybe this would soon be over and she could concentrate on finding a way to tell Frankie the truth about herself. She wouldn't think about that now. Now it was all about Gram.

"Well, well," a deep voice drawled as she turned on her heels. "If this isn't a coincidence. What are you doing down here all by yourself?" He laughed. "I swear, you're the icing on the cake, that's what you are." Jay Thurman stood on the ledge above the shore looking down at her. She unconsciously backed toward the river.

He jumped down the four-foot bluff in one

giant leap, landing with a reverberating thud seven feet away, more or less between her and her only escape route off the beach. He was dressed much as he had been two nights ago when she'd seen him in the car lights—jeans, a plaid shirt. His facial hair had grown even bushier and if anything, he looked more wired than he had before. Some kind of hot, jittery waves seemed to emanate from him.

"I'm sorry," she said, aware of the tremor in her voice. Her heart had sprung into her throat when he jumped and now stayed lodged there. "I'm sorry, but I really have to go," she said. "I'm late. If you'll excuse me…"

She took a step to the right and he followed suit. She stepped backward and then left. He grinned like a maniac as he mirrored her movements as though they were dancing.

"Listen," she said in her schoolteacher's stern voice. "Please move—"

"Or you'll what?" he said.

Her backpack lay behind him. What wouldn't she give to feel the handle of her machete gripped tightly in her hand? But her hands, like her pockets, were empty and he outweighed her by a hundred pounds. He seemed to sense the direction of her thoughts for he flexed bulging triceps.

"Please," she said, striving for control. "Someone is expecting me—"

Still smiling, he came another step closer. "Guess that someone is going to be disappointed," he said.

The thought of him grabbing her sent fear crawling over her skin like snakes. She stepped back toward the river and he followed suit. Then she pretended to step forward but instead twisted around and ran to the water. Almost at once, her feet started slipping on the mossy rocks but she managed to stay upright. Deeper, deeper, she had to get to water deep enough to carry her away, hopefully to the other side. She heard him wallow in after her. A second later, she thought she'd made it, but first one foot and then the other went out from under her and she landed with a splash, her butt hitting the rocks on the bottom, her hands scrambling to find something to grab on to, something to help pull herself into deeper water. Just as she finally felt the current lift her legs, Jay grabbed her hair and yanked her back. She screamed in both pain and outrage as he used her wet braid to drag her toward him and away from escape. Finally, with a heaving grunt, he hefted her weight up over his shoulder.

"You're going to pay for this," he growled, breathing hard as he lugged her out of the water and climbed the path with her still dangling over his shoulder. He smelled worse than a wet dog. She shifted her weight and kicked her legs in an effort to unbalance him. If he fell, she would have another chance to get away. But despite her efforts, he didn't falter. It was as though his shoes had spikes embedded in the soles.

"What do you want from me?" she demanded as he finally climbed onto the verge beside the dirt road and threw her to the rocky ground next to the old car she remembered from two nights before. She struggled into a sitting position as he stared at her.

He picked up a rock and weighed it in his hand, his gaze glued to her face, then he knelt on the ground beside her. Terrified, dripping wet, she faced him without flinching and repeated her question. "What do you want from me?"

"I want what's mine," he said and quick as lightning, slammed the rock down on her head.

FRANKIE TOOK OVER the combine for Chance who had promised to help Lily get supplies to the A-frame. He assured Frankie it would only take an hour or so and he'd tell Kate their plans for dinner if he saw her.

It was one of the longest hours Frankie had ever spent and he anticipated each moment of this day would drag in the same way as he waited for his father to return, spilled his guts and then went to face Jay.

How would Jay take the news that as far as Frankie was concerned, he could shout his threats from the rooftop?

Not well. If he couldn't get what he seemed so positive Frankie had and refused to share, then he would use violence. Frankie didn't doubt for a moment that Jay had tried blackmail first because it was easier, but violence would follow. All of a sudden, he wished he'd taken Kate home that morning.

But how did he run out on his family? There were currently three other women and now two children on this ranch. All of them were vulnerable, the men included. The ranch wasn't a fortress. That fact had been proven several times in the last year or so. Jay had to be stopped for good.

All these thoughts swirled in Frankie's head as he sat in the air-conditioned cab of the combine and mowed broad stretches of hay, row after row, with acres still to go. The tension inside his head began to build as Chance's predicted hour came and went. Finally, Frankie had had enough. He stopped the machine close to his truck and climbed down from the cab.

Pike pulled up alongside him and got out, too. "Something wrong?" he called.

"I need to go find Kate," he said. "I can't explain why—"

"You don't have to," Pike said. "I know just how you feel. Last winter when Sierra was in danger, I about went out of my mind. Go find Kate."

Frankie's cell phone rang before he could climb in his truck.

"Howdy," Jay said.

Frankie's face must have revealed how unhappy hearing this voice made him because he saw Pike straighten his shoulders and narrow his eyes.

"Jay," he said so Pike would know to whom he spoke.

"Time's up," Jay said.

"No, you gave me until ten—"

"I changed my mind. Oh, heck, where are my manners? Someone wants to talk to you."

The phone was dead for a second and then he heard Kate's voice. Weak and indistinct, she muttered, "Hello? Gram?"

All the air rushed out of his lungs. "Kate? Where are you? Are you okay?"

"I don't...know," she mumbled.

Jay came back on the line. "Poor little gal. Listen, pal, one of you is going to pay for the ten years I sat in a cell while you lived like a king. It's up to you to decide which one of you it is. Throw her under the bus like you did me or stand up for once?"

"Let her go. I'll do what you want," Frankie said immediately.

"There now, you're finally catching on. I'll call you back in fifteen minutes. You'd better have a plan for getting that gold today." The phone clicked off.

Frankie looked at Pike. "He's got Kate. He knew I wasn't going to fold so he took her."

"Do you know where?"

"No. He's calling back in fifteen minutes…." It wasn't enough time to call for help or try to trace a phone and no doubt it was a burner anyway. There wasn't enough time to do anything. He took off his hat and slammed it down on the ground. All he could think about was what he'd heard that afternoon about Jay raping Kara Richards years before. What depravity was he into now? His heart thundered and bellowed in his chest as he picked up his hat and shook the grass from its brim. His mind jumped around in his head like a steel sphere in a pinball machine.

"What are you going to do?" Pike asked.

"Get her back," Frankie muttered.

"How are you going to give him gold coins you don't have?"

Memories of Christmases long past popped into his head. "You have some, don't you? Remember, Grandma Hastings gave each of us gold coins every holiday for ten or twelve years. I sold mine to help make restitution to the man Jay shot during the robbery. But you still have a dozen or so, right?"

"Yeah. So do Gerard and Chance. They're yours, but—"

"Call Chance, better yet, go to his place. Go get the bank bags, get as many coins as you can, set up the cave to look like the bags have been sitting there for years but someone dragged off the gold, just like Chance said. Sprinkle some of the coins around, hide them in the dirt under footprints—whatever, just make it look like someone missed a few coins."

"Will thirty coins satisfy him?"

"Not forever, but maybe long enough to save Kate. I'll take Jay the long way around, tell him about another site, anything to stall. You and Chance go the shorter way, up the stream and across the plateau. Hurry, Pike, just do it, please."

Pike opened his truck, took a shotgun off the rack built in the back and shoved it at Frankie along with a box of ammo. Then he got in his truck and drove off across the field toward the road, the truck springs squeaking in protest on the uneven ground.

Frankie's phone rang. It had been less than five minutes.

"Well?" Jay said.

Obviously, Jay was trying to keep him off balance. It was working.

"You win," he said. "I'll trade gold for Kate."

"Good decision."

"Where do you want to make the handoff?"

"Handoff? I'm not crazy, you know." All traces of the folksy, phony humor gone now, replaced with a tone of superiority. "You get what you want when I get what I want."

Frankie had expected this. "At least tell me where she is."

"Not going to happen," Jay said. "For now she's safe. She'll be fine until I decide otherwise. You'll come with me so I can keep an eye on you." He paused for a second, his breathing heavy as though he was exerting himself. "I'll meet you in thirty minutes by the road to your little hideaway in the trees. Bring what equipment we'll need. I don't need to tell you to come alone and not to go whining to the cops, do I?"

"No," Frankie said right before the line went dead.

Did Jay still have Kate? Could she have gotten away from him—or was it possible his heavy breathing meant he'd been on the move when he called?

His mind created a dozen scenarios, each one worse than the last. Thoughts like these got him nowhere. He jumped in his truck and took off, punching in Pike's number as he drove. He didn't trust Jay as far as he could throw him. Thirty minutes could mean ten.

"Did you find Chance?" he asked when Pike answered.

"Yeah. He's getting those bank bags and the coins he still has. I'm at Gerard's house. He's offered his gold, too. I'll stop and get mine and we'll bypass the ghost town and go straight to the old cave. Try not to worry."

"Remind Gerard someone needs to make sure Lily and Grace and Kinsey and the rest are safe in case Jay goes off the deep end."

"Do you know where Jay lives? I could call the cops and get them searching."

"I don't have the slightest idea where he's taken her."

"Well, keep your cell on Vibrate. If by some miracle we find her or she wanders back on her own, I'll text you."

"I will."

Pike paused a second and added, "I've got to go, Frankie. Gerard's here with his coins. Hang in there, kid."

Chapter Seventeen

Kate drifted in and out of consciousness. When awake, she tried to figure out where she was, but with something tied over her head and her arms and legs bound to a chair, she couldn't place herself. That said, there was something in the back of her mind that told her she'd been here before.

It was hard to hold a thought, however, for along with consciousness also came waves of nausea and foreboding. She knew a strong man with rough hands had slapped her conscious and tied her up, but that's all she knew for sure. She thought she might have talked to someone else, but that could have been in a dream. Maybe it was Gram.

Panic rose in her throat like bile. Where was Gram? Who was looking after her? Was the front door locked?

And she remembered thinking she understood why she'd not been acting or feeling herself lately, but even that was fuzzy and tangled in with other thoughts and impressions. Maybe it had something to do with the fact that she was wet—her clothes, her hair...how did she get so wet?

FRANKIE RACED BACK to the main ranch house. He parked inside the barn and began piling equipment into the back of the truck.

As plans for recovering a supposedly long-buried treasure went, this seemed too far-fetched to convince even Jay, but he didn't know what else to do. He felt his only hope was to act with conviction. A moment later he was back in the truck and driving toward the road that led to his place, expecting to find Jay's old Pontiac parked beside the chain blocking off his road.

He had arrived first. He got out of the truck, too anxious to sit still, listening for the sound of an approaching motor. The only sounds he heard were the droning of insects and the distant sound of the river. As always, the river brought immediate gut-wrenching thoughts of Kate.

Kate. It always came back to her. Kate poking around the river, Kate asking questions but never answering any; beautiful, enigmatic, loving, secretive Kate. Kate, whom he had decided to trust with a lot more than a little beachfront property—he'd given her a chunk of his heart.

She couldn't be part of Jay's scheme, could she?

His head all but exploded at the thought. But the timing…no. No! He refused to believe it—this was desperation talking, this was fear.

"You're alone," Jay said and spooked Frankie so much he actually jumped. He spun around to face Jay who stood just a few feet away holding a tiny silver gun. The weapon looked way too small for Jay's beefy hand, which probably meant he'd stolen it. He would have had to, given his prison record.

Even more curious was how he had arrived so soundlessly.

"I'm alone," Frankie said.

"Got a gun?"

"In the back. An unloaded shotgun."

"Throw it out," Jay said.

"It might come in handy."

"Throw it out."

With Jay still pointing the gun right at his heart—it might be small, but he knew it would get the job done—Frankie set the unloaded shotgun well off the road. Jay did a quick pat down and, convinced Frankie was unarmed, directed him behind the wheel.

For a second, they sat side by side in the front

seat of the truck. The last time they'd done that the night had ended in disaster.

Frankie cleared his throat. "I'll try my best to help you," he said, "but tell me where Kate is."

Jay reached into his pocket and withdrew a small electronic device about the size of Frankie's cell phone. "This is a transmitter," he said. He turned it over so Frankie could see a tiny green light glowing in one corner. "As long as that light is green and steady, your girlfriend is alive and well. But if I push this button right here, it sends a signal, the light starts blinking, then it turns red and she's history."

"What have you done to her?" Frankie demanded.

Jay produced a creepy, leering smile. "For a time, I shared a cell with a guy they called the mad bomber. His motto was Retribution by Explosion. Your girl will never know what hit her but one minute she'll be a pretty little thing and the next she'll be a million pieces of bone and tissue." He put the device back in his pocket. "Okay, where's my gold?" He still held the gun pointed at Frankie.

Waves of anger had no place to go. Frankie had to shake them off, concentrate on the moment. "How did you know about the gold?" he asked. "And who convinced you I knew where it was?"

"I'm not answering any more questions."

"I'm asking because the truth is I'm not positive. If I knew who you spoke to—"

"Take it from me, buddy. You don't always get what you want. Get over it."

"Then we'll start with the Bowline River—"

"I warned you not to mess with me," Jay barked. One hand still clutched the tiny gun, but he'd buried the other deep in his pocket with the transmitter.

Relieved Jay wasn't interested in the river— surely that meant that Kate's agenda, whatever it was, did not tie in with Jay's—some of the tension leeched from his shoulders. "I was also told it might be in a cave up near the mine or it might be hidden in the ghost town itself," he said evenly. "In fact, damn near inside the actual bank from which it was stolen." He was betting Jay would prefer the ghost town. The Jay of a decade before had hated small, enclosed spaces.

"Might be?" Jay grumbled. "Come off it. I know you were told exactly where to search."

"I think your informant might have misled you. The truth is we were given three options," Frankie replied, meeting Jay's gaze straight on. He was making this up as he went along and knew he couldn't reveal even a trace of hesitation. "The river, the bank, the cave. If you'd waited, we would have narrowed things down. As it is...where do you want to look first?"

"Drive to the ghost town," Jay grumbled.

Frankie took off. To travel by vehicle meant crossing the river up near the main road and circling back across the southwest side of the plateau. The road wasn't used much except for fire equipment. The last time had been when Lily's estranged husband tried to torch what remained of Green Ridge several months before and Frankie's dad had driven a water truck up to stop the inferno.

Conversation in the truck was nonexistent. Jay was wired...nerves made his big body reek like sour milk. Frankie was afraid he'd say something that would reveal too much so he just kept his mouth closed.

Thirty minutes later, they pulled up outside the town limits of the ghost town. Each of them took an armload of tools out of the back and walked through a side street to access the bank.

Frankie hadn't been inside any of these buildings for a couple of years. The bank was especially unstable although it hadn't suffered any fire damage. He knew Gary Dodge wanted to film a portion of the documentary inside the building; in fact, Gary had discussed using a camera drone to make sure no human was hurt if the place came crashing down.

The second floor of the Green Ridge Bank, according to historians, had been used as offices and for storage but most of that floor had collapsed onto the first. Frankie hadn't realized the damage was so devastating and he approached the debris cautiously. They needed hard hats and bulldozers to excavate the building. The fiction Frankie had created about the gold being in this building was flimsy, at best.

However, in for a penny, in for a pound. He tapped this and that with a hammer, wrinkled his brow and shook his head. Finally, he announced they could move a few beams and some bricks and at least clear a section of floor.

As he worked, the mystery of this town and this bank seeped through his fear for Kate. The story of the robbery had always intrigued him—he'd read enough about the American West to know that men riding horses into town and stealing at gunpoint was more fiction than fact. In truth, there were few bank robberies, and by 1915, many areas of the country had switched payroll procedures. But that's how it had occurred in this little corner of nowhere and the story had always made his young heart beat faster. He supposed he always thought himself not so much as a member of the intrepid posse but of the thieves. His early foray into antisocial behavior had been as much imagination as reality.

Eventually, they found themselves looking down at dusty old floorboards. "Records say it could be hidden beneath these," Frankie said as he tackled cutting the boards to create an opening. A dark chasm loomed underneath. He knew what Jay didn't—there was no basement in this building, just a crawl space. He also knew Jay wouldn't trust Frankie to report what he found and despite his misgivings of tight, underground spaces, would force himself to accompany Frankie. If the bank chose the next fifteen minutes in which to collapse, they'd both be flatter than cow pies.

The good news was that all this hot, sweaty work had taken most of an hour and that would have given Chance and Pike an opportunity to prepare the cave. The bad news was the disturbing stillness of his phone. Kate must still be unaccounted for.

"You first," Jay said, motioning at the hole with his gun.

Frankie set the saw aside, rolled his shoulders, then picked up one of the lanterns he'd brought from the ranch. He let himself down into the crawl space. He wanted to corner Jay and overpower him in the worst possible way— what stopped him was the threat of that remote.

The crawl space turned out to be about two and a half feet high. Frankie doubted Jay would believe for a moment that someone had actually dug up the dirt to bury something down here. "Move out of the way," Jay said, now standing in the hole. Frankie moved. It was impossible not to feel the weight of the damaged building towering a few inches above his head. Jay's knees creaked as he lowered himself into a kneeling position. "Shine the light," he demanded.

Frankie did as directed but the light didn't go much farther than ten or twelve feet before running up against the rubble caused when the bank floor collapsed into the crawl space. Jay muttered a string of obscenities. Both men pulled themselves out of the hole.

"This is hopeless," Jay said, wiping his brow with the back of his arm.

"Yeah."

Jay's eyes narrowed and his jaw clenched as he apparently reviewed his options. The process looked painful. "We'll go check out that cave," he said. "There better be so much gold it burns my eyeballs or your little girlfriend is going to be sorry."

"No one hopes the damn gold is there more than me," Frankie said. Concern for Kate's safety gnawed at his gut—he'd never worried about anyone else like this. It was a terrible feeling made all the worse because this was his fault. Not only ten years ago when he didn't act responsibly, but ten hours ago when he made the decision to delay taking Kate to safety.

They dragged all the tools back down the alley and deposited them in the truck bed. Frankie got behind the wheel again and because he knew he was a lot more familiar with this area than Jay was, felt safe taking the long way around to the other side of Green Peak to eat up a little more time.

He and his brothers had found this cave twenty-five years earlier although it had probably been discovered by others in the years preceding that. As Frankie recalled, it started out very narrow, more like a slit in the rocks than a hole. After four or five feet of that, it opened up a bit and eventually erupted through a tunnel of sorts into a cavern beyond. This was where he and Chance always expected to find a hibernating bear, something Frankie now found terribly naive. How could a bear have made it through the first narrow gap?

It was midafternoon by the time they approached the cave. Frankie saw no sign of his brothers; indeed, it didn't look like anyone had been here in years and for a heart-stopping moment, he wondered if something had gone wrong and they hadn't come.

"How would someone get bags of gold in there?" Jay grumbled.

"One at a time," Frankie said. "Makes it a perfect hiding spot, though."

"There's probably bats or spiders," Jay said.

"And maybe gold."

"You go first but I want to see at least part of you." He jiggled his pocket before adding, "And remember. One little push and poof, the girl is toast."

"I'm not likely to forget," Frankie said and immediately sidled through the vertical crevice created by the rocks, keeping his shoulders back and his head turned to the side. A shovel and lantern dangled down by his legs. Jay had the pickax and another lantern. As Frankie investigated the cramped area leading to the tunnel up ahead through which they'd have to crawl, he heard Jay puffing and swearing. What if he got stuck? Would he panic and hit the remote? Frankie grabbed his arm and pulled on it until, like a cork from a bottle, Jay all but popped out of the crevice.

More swearing.

"Come on," Frankie said after a few seconds. "It's got to be close now. And remember, we're splitting fifty-fifty. You can take your half with you, but mine stays here until the documentary."

"Sure," Jay said.

Clearly, he had no intention of honoring that part of his deal. It was academic, of course, because there was no gold but it underscored the man's ruthlessness. He wouldn't leave Frankie—or Kate—to report him. Frankie had to make sure he not only got out of this cave but he somehow got that transmitter. "Looks like it's hands and knees up ahead," he said.

"Go first," Jay demanded, once again making a big deal of fidgeting with his pocket.

Frankie crawled through the tunnel, pushing the light ahead of him, trailing the shovel behind. It was roomier than the crevice and didn't last long before it turned into a space about the size of an empty train car.

It was much as Frankie remembered it from childhood: dark, claustrophobic. There was a second when he could have brought the shovel down on Jay's emerging head. Only fear of that damn button stilled his hands.

As Jay finished heaving himself through the tunnel, the light from Frankie's lantern caught the dingy, yellowing white of the ancient bank bags Chance and Pike had staged in a far corner. This was it.

"I see something," he said, once again pulling on Jay's arm and doing his best to sound excited.

Jay needed no further encouragement. He got

to his feet, his eyes growing big as he registered a heap of bulging bank bags.

Bulging?

For a second, Frankie wondered if they'd actually found the lost coins and he worked at wrapping his head around the coincidence of it all. But as he moved closer he saw that the bags—and there were only a dozen or so—were really full of rocks. Other bags were empty and half-buried in the dry, sandy floor of the cave. Everything looked like it had been there for decades.

Jay played his light over what he'd hoped would be a fortune. "What happened to my gold?" he shouted.

Frankie shook his head. The desperation of the plan now struck him full in the face. One moment of anger and Kate could die. The little silver gun, which Frankie hadn't seen in a while, suddenly made a return appearance. *Shoot me*, he urged silently. *Just don't push the button.*

"Empty those bags," Jay demanded, and Frankie overturned the nearest one onto the ground. For the life of him, he could see no coins. Had Chance and Pike been here? Had they misunderstood when and where to go but if so, where did these bags come from?

A bunch of rocks—exactly like those that

lay scattered on the ground, tumbled out of the old bank bag.

"I don't get it," Jay whispered. "What happened?"

Frankie didn't have to work hard to look scared, dumbstruck, anxious...no acting skills required. "I think it must have been stolen after it was hidden," he said slowly. "A long time ago, I mean. Maybe the fourth man, the one who got away, maybe he came back for it when his friends had been killed and the heat was off. Look," he added, running the light along the cave floor. "It appears someone dragged a heavy load across here through the tunnel."

"But why put rocks in the bags?"

Good question. "I don't know," Frankie said.

"Maybe whoever took the coins was planning on fooling someone," Jay said. "Maybe this happened years later, maybe a couple of guys, guys like you and me made a deal like the one we made and one tried to cheat the other." He turned his attention to Frankie and studied his face in the indirect light.

"I guess we'll never know," Frankie said, his mouth dry. For a moment, he thought the game was over. Jay's fingers tightened on the pistol grip, his mouth turned down at the corners, his eyes narrowed to slits. He looked over Frankie's shoulder at what he'd imagined would be a ton of gold to plunder but turned out to be a bunch of nothing and Frankie could feel the other man's blood pressure getting ready to explode like a geyser. And then Jay made a small whooping noise.

"What's that?" he said, and dropped to his knees. He scratched at the dirt for a second before holding up a small gold coin. An almost imperceptible gasp of relief escaped Frankie's lips as Jay held it up to admire. Pike and Chance must have been here—there was still a possibility this could work.

"I guess whoever did this missed one," Jay said. He got to his feet and once again pointed the gun at Frankie. "Empty every bag, search the floor. I want every coin the bastard left behind."

Frankie upended all the bags, almost certain Chance had filled them. He could almost see his brother's grin as he imagined Jay's greedy gaze lingering over what appeared to be bulging bags of loot.

One coin tumbled out of the last bag. Jay grabbed for it as Frankie began searching the rest of the floor. He soon wished his brothers hadn't been quite so thorough at hiding the coins. He wasn't positive exactly how many they'd left here, but he eventually found thirty-six. He hoped to high heaven that their mint dates were old enough to make them believable although he really didn't care once Kate was safe. Jay could threaten and rage all he wanted once he had no hostage. He'd broken parole by carrying a weapon to say nothing of attempted blackmail and kidnapping. Jay was on his way back to jail whether or not he killed Frankie and Kate. Chance and Pike would see to that.

"Let's get out of here," Jay said.

"Give me the remote," Frankie countered.

"Not yet."

"I brought you to the coins like I said I would."

"Thirty-six lousy dollar coins, worth what, a couple thousand bucks? Big deal."

"That's not my fault," Frankie said. "And it's not Kate's. Keep your part of the bargain—give her back safe and sound."

"You're going to drive me to my car," Jay insisted. "Once I'm on my way, I'll tell you where she is."

"At least disable the remote."

"No. I don't trust you. This all seems like a setup to me. You haven't heard the last of me."

"Jay, I don't know what more I can do. I don't know where there's any more gold. If I did, you'd be welcome to it. All I want is Kate. You took a chance, it didn't pay off. Like you said, you don't always get what you want."

Jay reached into his pocket and withdrew the

remote transmitter. His thumb quivered above the button…

"I'll find some way to pay you, just not in gold," Frankie said quickly. "My dad's rich, you said so yourself. I just want you to go away, that's all. Leave Kate and me alone and go far, far away."

He didn't like the gleam in Jay's eyes.

Jay's thumb stopped hovering. "You go first," he said, motioning toward the tunnel.

Frankie got down on his hands and knees, and much as he'd entered, left the bigger part of the cave, Jay on his heels. They both got to their feet as soon as possible. Jay held the remote in one hand and the tiny gun in his other. The time to act would be when they emerged from the cave. Frankie had to be ready. He started to go first again, but Jay put out an arm to stop him. "Stay here 'til I yell for you to come. I'm going first this time." He entered with the remote hand giving Frankie no opportunity to grab it.

Eventually, he heard Jay yell and he made his way through the crevice, wincing as the sun hit his face.

As he shaded his eyes against the brilliance, Jay shoved the gun against his forehead. "You double-crossed me," he said as though he'd had time to think about the past two hours more carefully.

"If there was a double cross, don't look any farther than the person who told you I was positive where to find the gold," Frankie said.

Jay dropped the gun and produced the remote. "I think it's time you suffered like I suffered. Time for you to lose for a change."

At that exact moment, the unmistakable sound of gunfire rent the air. Startled, Frankie dived to the ground. He looked at Jay in time to see the big man clutch the remote to his chest and then collapse onto the ground.

"No!" Frankie yelled, the word yanked from his chest as though it was his heart. "Stop firing," he yelled toward the trees as he scrambled to Jay's side. He could see no one about but in truth, he wasn't looking, his attention was focused solely on Jay Thurman's unmoving body. The bullet had obviously exited through his back; his shirt was soaked in bright red blood that had splattered all over the rock behind him.

Frankie tugged him over.

"Is he dead?" someone yelled as Frankie delicately uncurled Jay's bloody fingers from around the remote. "Is it safe now?"

Frankie couldn't respond. His mouth felt like

a clay oven, his heart raced. The blinking red light on Jay's remote penetrated his brain.

It was too late. He'd failed. The bomb had been detonated.

Chapter Eighteen

Pat Lowell came to a halt a few feet in front of Frankie and stared down at the man he'd just killed with the scoped rifle he held in his hands. "What made him think there was gold here?" he demanded. "Thank goodness I came along in time."

Frankie didn't trust himself to talk. He couldn't make sense of anything. What was their historian doing here? Why had he shot Jay? He ignored Pat and got to his feet as Pike and Chance appeared, both out of breath like they'd been running. "What happened?" demanded Pike.

"I had no choice," Pat said. "The brute raised that black thing in his hand and I thought it was a gun. He was going to kill Frankie."

"That thing is a remote connected to a bomb set to explode to kill Kate," Frankie said, his voice as dead as his heart. "He activated it when you shot him."

"What?" Pat turned to Chance and Pike. "I didn't know. No one told me..."

"No one knew," Chance said. He knelt by Jay's body and dug in his pocket, extracting a set of car keys. A few of the gold coins recovered in the cave fell unheeded to the ground. Frankie hated the sight of them and turned his back.

His mind raced. How had Jay approached him near the Keep Out sign without being heard? He'd parked close by and walked, that's how. It was the only answer. And the only place to park out of sight was near Frankie's own tree house and that meant he'd been there the whole time, waiting for Frankie. And that could be where he'd stashed Kate. There might be a chance the bomb misfired or that there never was a bomb in the first place.

"Come on," he yelled, grabbing the car keys from Chance's hand. Such was the desperation in his voice that Pat and Chance piled into the back of Frankie's truck without asking why. Frankie got behind the wheel and Pike jumped in beside him right as Frankie shifted the truck into Reverse, backed around and took off toward the ranch.

He was way too preoccupied to talk. There

was no point in talking anyway. If Jay had stashed Kate in his car and then blown it up, she was dead. She didn't feel dead to him. He wouldn't believe it until he had no other option. He could not fail her, he just couldn't.

He stopped the truck while Chance jumped out and undid the chain, then jumped back onto the rear bumper as Frankie tore off down his road.

Even before he saw Jay's old Pontiac still in one piece and squatting in the clearing, Frankie smelled smoke. He slammed on the brakes and jumped out of the truck, immediately breaking into a run. The tree house was on fire.

Pike thundered on his heels. "The bathhouse," Frankie yelled. He kept a few fire extinguishers down there. Pike would find them. He took off up the ramp. The smoke grew increasingly dense as flames licked through the roof and had started in on the branches above. He tore off his shirt and used it to grab the door handle, almost wrenching it out of the frame.

"Kate!" he yelled but heard nothing. He could see open flames licking at the walls near the kitchen area and knew time was short before the whole place went up like a tinderbox. His mind took in a dozen other details he didn't register. For now he was struck with the urgency of finding Kate. He heard a noise near the floor and dropped to his knees where vision was marginally better and the air more breathable. That's where he found Kate although he couldn't swear it was her as there was a sack of some kind tied over her head. She was tied to a chair. His knife was out of his pocket in one second and slicing through the bonds in another. He lifted her over his shoulder and carried her toward the door as Pike showed up with a fire extinguisher. Frankie hurried down the ramp with Kate, moving far enough along the road to get her out of the worst of the smoke.

He noticed that Chance and Pat Lowell had taken the truck, probably to get additional equipment. For now, he contented himself with removing the bag that covered Kate's head. Her face was very pink and dotted with sweat. Her eyes rolled open and she stared at him without really seeing him. He touched her throat and felt her heartbeat. It was fast, but it was also steady. He didn't know he was crying until he felt cool tears slide down his charred cheeks.

Pike showed up a minute later. "It's too big to put out with an extinguisher. I've called the fire department. Where's your water supply?

"Behind the bathhouse. There's a hose back there and the water feeds directly from the river. I'm staying with Kate."

Pike took a step back toward the tree house

and then paused. "There's something you need to know. Gerard told me that Kinsey said Kate might be pregnant. She wanted us to know in case Kate was hurt. An ambulance is on its way."

Frankie nodded. Kate? Pregnant? They'd deal with that later. He picked her up and carried her farther away from the fire before putting her down again. Glancing over his shoulder, he saw the fire had spread to other trees. He brought her hand up to his face and kissed her fingers. His reward was that she opened her eyes again, and this time her focus seemed steadier.

"Gram?" she whispered. "Where's my grandmother? What have you done with her?"

Then she fainted.

"Thurman rigged a pretty simple bomb and left it in your house," Officer Rob Hendricks told Frankie that evening. "We gather he brought Ms. West back when he came across her on the beach. Anyway, the fire marshal says the bomb shorted out when the signal was sent. The milk carton he'd assembled it in caught fire and then the fire spread. The house is gone. You lost several trees along a path down toward the river, as well. We're lucky it stopped when it got to your road." He looked down at Kate and added, "That was smart of you to tip your chair over so you'd be down on the floor where the air was better," he said.

"I'm not sure when the chair fell over," Kate said. "It might have been an accident. When it comes to the fire, everything before Frankie uncovering my face is kind of a blur."

"Is it all still a blur?" Frankie asked.

"No. It's coming back now."

Rob started writing down Kate's story of the abduction and waking up when Jay slapped her. If Jay hadn't already been dead, Frankie would have left the room to hunt him down.

But she was also kind of evasive when it came to saying what part of the river she'd been on when Jay found her. And she said he'd acted surprised to see her and taunted her about being the icing on the cake. Hendricks let most of this slip—Jay was dead, there wasn't a doubt in anyone's mind that he'd set himself up for disaster or that Kate had nothing to do with it so perhaps all the questions were more or less a formality.

Rob was a longtime friend of the family and his interview style was professional. He'd been Gerard's best man at his first wedding, but he'd also been on duty the night Frankie turned himself in after the convenience store robbery and this had created an awkwardness between them through the years. When Kate had finished, Rob shook Frankie's hand. "I'm really glad this ended well for both of you," he said before he left.

"Alone at last," Frankie quipped as he sat on a chair pulled up beside her bed and took Kate's hand. "How does your head feel? You have a charming bump."

She smiled. "I'm okay," she said.

He leaned over her face and kissed her cheek. Her long hair lay on the pillow around her head and smelled of smoke, but she looked beautiful.

"I need to call my grandmother," she said. "It seems like I haven't heard from her in weeks."

"You talked to Pine Hill this morning, but while I was waiting for the doctor to finish examining you, I went ahead and called them again. You'd used my phone so it was in the record."

"Thank you for doing that. What did they say?"

"They were real positive. Said she was eating a little better and had actually hummed along with a tune someone played on the piano."

"Wow. That's great, isn't it?"

"Yes it is. They were alarmed to hear you'd been in a fire and urged me to tell you your grandmother is fine, just take care of yourself."

Her smile faded a bit. "Frankie, there are things I need to tell you."

"Like the fact you may be pregnant?"

"That and—wait, how did you know?"

"Kinsey warned Gerard in case you were injured. Gerard told Pike. Pike told me."

"I wasn't sure but they did a test when I got here."

"And?"

Tears filled her eyes as she nodded. "They're not sure if the smoke and everything hurt the baby. I could lose him or her."

"How do you feel about that?"

"I guess a lot of people would feel relieved, but today when Jay was tossing me around, I realized I want this child. The timing is terrible, but—"

"I understand. Is it Luke's baby?"

She nodded.

"This will be his legacy," Frankie said.

"But Luke has family," she added. "Parents and a brother who will want to know his son or daughter."

"Of course they will."

"So if you and I…if we…well, I guess I'm trying to say that I know you dreamed of your children all having the same parents. That can't happen if I have this baby. I understand if you—"

"Wait just a second," he said. "That wasn't a dream, Kate. That was a plan. Plans are flexible. The only real dream I have at this moment is that we continue what we've started. I don't want to lose you."

"Like you lost your beautiful tree house."

"The next tree house I build will be for a child," he said, touching her belly gently.

The nurse found them several minutes later, Frankie sitting on the edge of the bed, Kate in his arms, their lips locked together.

"Now, now, you two," she said with a laugh. "Take it on home, okay?"

Frankie smiled at her. As he helped Kate with her shoes, he looked up at her face. "Was there something else you wanted to talk to me about?" he asked.

She met his gaze, then shook her head. "It can wait," she said.

"WHAT DO YOU mean Pat's gone?" Frankie asked Pike after they returned to the ranch house.

"He drove in to Falls Bluff to be interviewed by the police. He'll be back tomorrow," Pike said.

"I don't get what he was doing here in the first place," Frankie said. "And how in the world did he end up at the cave?"

"He was on his way to Boise. The expert he had looking at those letters wants a face-to-face talk with him to discuss the results. When he didn't find anyone at the main house, he drove up to Gerard's. Gerard told him what was going on. He said he wanted to help and took off. Gerard called Chance to tell him to expect Pat. But Pat didn't show up. We were waiting down the hill when we saw him drive past us toward the cave. By the time we caught up to head him off, he had disappeared into the trees and then I guess he saw you and Jay and decided to be a hero."

"And almost got Kate killed," Frankie said, his hand closing protectively on her shoulder. He was standing behind her chair and she tilted her head back to look up at him.

"Lucky for me I had a hero of my own," she said.

The door opened and Harry Hastings, looking tired from a full day of driving, entered from the mudroom.

"Did you get the part?" Pike asked.

"No. They read the damn serial number wrong over the phone and I went all that way for nothing. What did you guys get done today?"

Frankie and Pike looked at each other, then at their father. "I need to talk to you about that," he said. "Let's go into the office for a little while."

"If there's a glass of scotch waiting for me when I get there, I'm all ears," Harry said, and sighed.

Frankie leaned down and kissed the top of Kate's head. "I'll see you later."

KATE KNEW SHE had to retrieve her backpack from the river before someone else found it. Frankie was busy with his dad. She could be back here within an hour. All she needed to do was get her hands on a flashlight and wait for Pike to leave the house.

"I have good news," Pike said as he got up from his chair. He walked to the sink and rinsed out the glass from which he'd been drinking. "My fiancée, Sierra, is arriving tomorrow for a weeklong stay."

"That's great," Kate said.

"You'll still be here, right?"

"In all honesty, I'm anxious to get back to my grandmother but I'll be here through tomorrow."

"Good. Sierra's looking forward to meeting you."

They smiled at each other. Kate was surprised Sierra even knew she existed. Pike had probably told his fiancée that a woman determined to fight the documentary was visiting—just another example of the shame she would have to face when the truth came out.

"You okay?" Pike asked.

"Tired. I think I'll take a shower and call it a night."

"Sounds good," he said. "I was just hanging around in case you wanted company."

She touched his arm. "Thank you, Pike—for

everything. I'll see you tomorrow." A moment later, the outside door closed behind him. Kate waited until she heard his vehicle climb the hill outside, then she grabbed a flashlight from the barn and headed toward the bridge.

Jay was dead—there was nothing to be afraid of. The dark was just night, nothing more. No boogeymen, no fire, no fear. Get the backpack, get back to her room, take a shower and figure out what to do tomorrow, her last day on the ranch.

It was either farther than she remembered or she was a lot more tired and soon she began to wish she'd taken a horse. The real reason she hadn't was that she didn't want to get caught out here by Frankie or another Hastings and have to explain what she was doing with the pack. She figured that on foot she'd have time to ditch it if she saw lights or heard voices and could claim a restless walk.

Boy, was she sick of all this pretending.

The smell of burned wood assaulted her nose and, with regret, she thought of the beautiful house Frankie had lost. He'd shrugged that loss off, but it had to hurt.

The backpack was right where she'd dropped it. She shrugged it on and turned to leave, but instead swiveled to face west. The rock, bathed in moonlight, looked more like a woman wearing a hat than it had in the bright light of day. Her heartbeat doubled. If she got out here early enough, she could find the jewels and then talk to Frankie. Perhaps if she showed her find to him instead of slinking away with it, he'd understand.

Shivers overtook her as she stood there and she twirled around, sure she was going to find Jay standing above her. Nothing there, of course, just memories. Time to go. She hadn't even cleared Frankie's road when she spotted lights approaching and quickly tossed the pack beneath the bushes as she kept walking.

The lights blinded her and she stopped to shade her face. Frankie got out of his truck. "I thought I might find you out here. Everything okay?"

"Fine," she said. "I'm just restless."

"Tomorrow is the big day," he said and for a second she wasn't sure what he meant. Had he figured her out? "Gary and Pat are both going to be here early in the morning. The expert came through with a location out by Ten Cent Creek. By tomorrow afternoon, we should know if we have a great end for the documentary or not."

"The irony of all that gold being hidden in a place called Ten Cent Creek is pretty sweet," she said.

He chuckled.

"I take it the talk with your father went okay?"

"He knew all about it, Kate. He's been waiting years for me to get it off my chest, said he'd just about given up hope I ever would. The old man surprised me."

"Do you feel better?"

"What's the saying? The truth will set you free? So, yes, I do feel better."

The truth will set you free. She stared into his eyes, eyes that glittered in the ambient light of the headlamps off to their side, eyes that shone with affection—affection for her. All she wanted in the world at that moment was to fall into his arms, his bed, his future. "I have something I have to tell you," she said softly, gripping his hands and holding them tightly.

"Is it about your interest in the Bowline River?" he asked.

"Yes. But it's also about the lies I've told you—"

"Lies?" he interrupted. "What are you talking about?"

She swallowed hard. This was it. "I came here under false pretenses, Frankie. I've been lying to you since the day we met. I let you think you invited me here—"

He shook his head, his expression confused. "You've been lying to me?"

"Yes. I'm so sorry. I needed to come here for my grandmother's sake. See—"

"What does your grandmother have to do with you coming here?"

"Everything."

"The whole thing about the documentary—"

"A lie," she whispered.

He stared at her like he'd never seen her before. "Are you really even Kate West?"

"Of course. And Gram is my grandmother. Almost all the personal things I told you are true."

"Almost?" he said, and pulling his hands from hers, took a step back. "I don't understand."

"I know. I'm trying to tell you. The things that have passed between us are real. Just calm down and listen."

"Don't tell me to calm down," he said raising his voice. Jaw set, he hitched his hands on his waist and studied the ground for a moment, then he looked back at her. "Were you in cahoots with Jay Thurman?"

"How could you ask me such a thing?"

"You were down here when he 'found' you, weren't you?"

"It was a fluke. I had nothing to do with Jay. I'm trying to find something—"

"Gold?"

"No, diamonds."

"Diamonds!"

"They were stolen back when the bank was robbed."

"What are you talking about? There were no diamonds—"

"Yes, there were. The man who lost them decided to keep it quiet. The bank wasn't anxious to admit personal property had disappeared either, so—"

"This is gibberish," Frankie said, taking another step away.

"—so it never came out. Those diamonds actually belong to my grandmother now, Frankie. My grandfather was related to the man who lost them."

The seconds ticked by as he stared at her. "Is this the truth or another lie?"

She took a shaky breath. "It's the truth."

"So, you're here to what? Steal diamonds?"

"No, not steal them."

"Right," he said with sarcasm. "That's why you've been so up-front with everyone. That's why you've been sneaking around. You had no intention of ever telling me any of this, did you?"

"No," she admitted, no longer looking in his eyes. They were mere slits now and whatever she'd seen sparkling in them five minutes before had gone away.

"I should have known it was all too good to be true," he said in a voice that broke her heart.

"What do you mean?" she asked.

"Us. You. All too fast…all too perfect."

"Frankie," she pleaded. "Please, I know you're angry—"

"Stop," he said and she raised her gaze at the tone of his voice. "Yeah, I'm angry. I feel used and I've only really felt that way once before when Jay—but, I'm also disappointed. I would hope by now that you'd recognize my priorities. What's important to me on this ranch are the people. If you'd only confided in me."

"I wanted to," she almost whispered.

"Then why didn't you?"

"I need these diamonds for my grandmother's safety. How could I possibly risk that based on the trust I began to feel for a man I was falling in love with? What if I was mistaken?"

He shook his head. "We all make mistakes," he said as though he'd almost made a huge one by believing in her. He looked toward the river then back at her. "I can't talk about this anymore tonight. I don't want to say things I'll regret. I need time to process what you've told me. Let me get through tomorrow morning and then we'll figure this out. Get in the truck and I'll give you a ride back to the ranch."

"I can walk—"

"I'm not leaving you alone out here," he said. She wasn't sure how he meant that and she didn't ask. She agreed with him: they'd both already said enough. She got in the truck.

Chapter Nineteen

Frankie loitered in the kitchen the next morning, waiting for Kate to appear. Gary Dodge, Pat Lowell, his dad and brothers were all out loading ATVs onto trailers they could use when they got to Ten Cent Creek. Gary had brought a bunch of cameras and digging equipment so they'd ruled out horses as transport. Grace had walked up to spend the morning with Kinsey. Lily and Charlie were both sleeping in since today was an in-service day at his school and there were no classes.

Kate finally appeared. He darted her a quick glance but it was long enough to tell she'd rested about as good as he had, which wasn't saying much.

"I waited for you," he said.

She nodded.

Was he still angry and hurt? Yes. Did he still yearn to see her smile, to wipe the worry out of her eyes? Yes to that, too. It was like being caught in a whirlpool, emotions spinning him around. "Kate, I don't want to go off worrying about whether you'll be here when I get back," he said and meant it.

"I wouldn't leave like that," she said.

"I hope not. Please, wait until this is over to do anything."

"I have to continue looking, Frankie. Nothing has changed about the diamonds except I'll have to prove they belong to Gram."

"You're a one note song on that matter," he said.

"I know. I have to be."

"Then let's compromise. I'll help you find them when I get back."

Tears gathered in her eyes and she flicked them away with her fingertips.

He gripped her shoulders. "Don't cry," he said with a swift glance.

"I'm just so ashamed," she whispered. "Are you ever going to be able to look directly at me again?"

"I hope so," he said with more honesty than either of them could bear. He leaned forward and kissed her forehead. "Just wait for me," he added. A horn honked outside and he tore himself away from her. It was time to shift gears and try to concentrate on buried treasure.

KATE SADDLED GINGER and rode her across the bridge, her goal to reclaim the backpack she'd ditched last night. This was the first morning in her life that she'd awoken knowing she carried a new life and the weight of that tiny responsibility had actually made everything clear.

A baby meant the future and though parts of hers were troubling, parts were sad and parts were devastating with their potential for loss, it was that future that mattered.

Seeing Frankie this morning had reminded her of the flip side of the saying he'd used the night before. The truth may set you free, but it doesn't always set everybody else free. She'd caused him a lot of self-doubt and pain and for that she was truly sorry. If he gave her a chance, she would try to make it up to him—it depended on him now.

Eventually, she found the ungainly pack where she'd thrown it in the underbrush and strapped it to Ginger's back. The beach was right up ahead, and curious to see the rock in the light of day, she rode on. Once there, she looped Ginger's reins over a branch and made her way down the trail. The sun had burned away Jay's ghost and she felt no foreboding, just rampant curiosity. On a whim, she trotted back up to Ginger and took her pack off the back of the saddle. Frankie had asked her to wait for him, but here she was and she found she couldn't. It wouldn't hurt to look around a little…

Down on the beach again, she reviewed what Greg Abernathy had told her as she unpacked her tools. She approached the rock slowly and circled it.

How did you bury something in a rock? You didn't, not without tools or explosives. It had been done on the run so presumably whoever hid the diamonds hadn't had climbing equipment and, besides, the rock had been in the water at the time. It must be that the mountaintop lining up with the boulder and the snagged tree that had existed at the time created a landmark. She turned to look behind her and almost fell over.

The fire had cleared a clear path back to where Frankie's house had once hovered in the boughs. And now visible through that gap was the top of an old, charred, snagged tree.

She moved to align herself and walked toward the verge, swinging her machete, climbing the rise of the bank carefully as she fought the inevitable vines. She did this for several moments until the ground evened out. Yesterday's fire had come within fifty feet and the vines here had shriveled from the heat. She swung the machete at the largest clump. It stopped abruptly as it hit rock, the impact vibrating up her arm.

Quickly, she cleared as much undergrowth as possible until she revealed the unmistakable circular shape of a crumbling old well. Once, there had been a house nearby, but that had burned to the ground before the robbery. The well had been abandoned for well over a century. Was it the hiding spot? She shone a light in the middle of the formation and discovered rocks had been piled inside the three-foot circle to within a foot of its rim. They may have been part of a collapse or they may have been put there. She glanced back at the river—this close to water, a well wouldn't have to be deep. The diamonds could be closer than she dared to dream.

There was only one way to find out.

"I WANT YOU to know how grateful I am that my rash actions yesterday didn't result in a tragedy for Kate West," Pat Lowell told Frankie as they unpacked gear from the back of a trailer.

"I appreciate that," Frankie said.

Pat was dressed as he always was, in a button-down shirt, this one bright blue, and tweed pants. He looked about as out of place in a field of livestock as was possible. He had used the notes the expert made to direct them to a small grove of trees close to the creek that would be three times as wide come winter. Horses and cattle watched the goings-on from a distance as Pike, Chance and Gary began digging in the rocky earth.

"I guess it wouldn't have happened at all if she'd only been here the day or two she originally planned," Pat added.

"I guess not," Frankie said. He set a stack of shoring lumber aside and narrowed his eyes. "Let me ask you a question. In all your investigations did you ever come up with any data or rumor about diamonds being stolen along with the gold?"

Pat's forehead furrowed. "Diamonds? What do you mean?"

"Loose diamonds, I guess. I'm not sure."

"There was zero mention of diamonds," Pat said firmly. "Why do you ask?"

Frankie shook his head. "Maybe she's still lying," he muttered.

"What? Who?"

"Nothing," Frankie said quickly. "Excuse me, I think I better go help Pike and Gary dig." He stalked off, wanting desperately to believe Kate and yet wondering if he was a fool to do so. He'd bet his left arm she was down at the river right that moment despite him having asked her to wait for him.

For two hours, he worked out his mixed-up feelings by attacking the ground with a shovel, widening the hole until it began to fill with water. "This is impossible," Gary finally said as mud oozed over his boots. "Let's take a break. We need to ask Pat if there's any indication in the expert's notes that will help us narrow the search."

They all paused to wash off in the creek. Frankie took off his shirt, dipped it in the water and wrung it out before putting it back on. It felt great against his overheated skin.

"Where's Pat?" he asked when he caught up with the other guys grabbing sodas from an ice chest.

"Dad said he felt a migraine coming on," Pike said. "It appears he took the notes with him so now we're playing a waiting game while he drives back to the house to get his medicine."

"I didn't know Pat had migraines," Frankie said. He looked at Gary. "Did you?"

"First time I've heard anything about it," Gary said.

As they sat on the edge of the trailers discussing their options, Frankie's mind wandered immediately to Kate—no surprise there.

Twenty-four hours ago, he would have moved heaven and earth to save her from Jay. He'd known exactly how he felt about her. And now?

What had she said last night? Something about not trusting him with the truth because she'd been falling in love with him. But last night she had spilled her guts—did that mean what he thought it meant? Did that mean she knew she was in love now?

And how did he feel about that?

"I'm going to go check on Pat," Frankie said because he didn't want to announce he wanted—he needed—to see Kate. This was 90 percent his project and walking out in the middle of it went against every instinct except one and that's the one Frankie couldn't ignore.

He was in love with Kate West. Upset with her, yes, that too, but in love. He'd been in love with her since first glance. He'd known it, too, he'd *felt* it.

Who was he to condemn her for being scared and telling a lie when to her, at first, he was a complete stranger? He'd done the same thing to his own father. He'd bet the ranch she didn't have a shred of evidence to prove the diamonds—if there were diamonds—were legally hers. She'd probably caught some rambling of her grandmother's or gossip passed from one relative to another and been desperate enough to move heaven and earth to try to find a way to save her grandmother's house. The bottom line was everything important about her rang true in the deepest recesses of his heart.

Now that he'd turned this corner in his head, he was anxious to share the news with Kate.

He drove past the road that had once led to his tree house but as he passed it by, he slowed down. There had been a dust trail hanging in the still air and that made him curious. Had the fire restarted? Was Kate down at the part of the river where he'd come across her last night? He backed up and started down his road until he saw the back end of a red SUV pulled behind some trees. That was Pat's car—what was he doing out here? He parked next to it and looked inside in case the man had passed out or something. The car was empty.

He stood there a second until he heard the unmistakable sound of a horse approaching and turned quickly. Ginger wandered up to him, her saddle empty, reins dragging on the ground. There was no way to tell who'd been riding her but it was obvious whoever they were had been left behind and he couldn't imagine the horse had a thing to do with it. Chances were good this horse had been with Kate—so where was Kate?

He slipped off the saddle and bridle, dumped them in the back of his truck and sent Ginger on her way. Then he walked down the road. Reason said Kate might have fallen so he kept his eyes peeled. There was nothing to suggest she was in trouble. The sound of rock hitting rock finally reached his ears and it actually relaxed him a little as he vividly recalled the way she'd hacked at the rocks on the other side of the river. He'd known her curiosity would drive her down here!

But what did Pat have to do with anything?

That question turned more important when Frankie rounded the curve in the road and caught sight of a blue shirt and tweed pants. Pat stood very still up ahead, his back to Frankie, peering through the branches of the remaining stand of trees that had escaped the wrath of the fire.

He was about to call out to Pat and ask what was going on when Pat moved into the trees. The way he did it was so stealthy it couldn't help but arouse suspicion. A sudden whoop up ahead sounded excited. Pat paused midstep at the sound and Frankie drew back toward the shadows. He knew it was Kate's voice. Was it possible there really were diamonds and she'd just found them?

Pat was on the move again. A few seconds later he called out. "Kate? I've been looking for you!"

Frankie crept up to where Pat had stood a few moments before and found an unobstructed view of Kate standing in a clearing, up to her waist inside a circular depression. Dozens of toaster-sized rocks lay on the ground outside the perimeter and that explained what he'd been hearing. She'd been lifting rocks out of the old well.

Was that a good thing for a pregnant woman to do? Why hadn't she waited for him?

"Mr. Abernathy!" Kate said. "What are you doing here? Is it Gram?"

"No, no," Pat said as he walked into view. "I checked on her a couple of days ago—she's fine. I just got to thinking of you out here all by yourself. Thought I'd help." He paused before adding, "What's that you're holding? Did you find the diamonds?"

"I'm not sure. There's some rotting clothes in here and boots, too. No bones but I just found this saddlebag and my hopes are high," she added.

"Let's get you out of that hole," he said, extending a hand. "I'll take that old thing."

She handed him the saddlebag before climbing out of the well. Holding it gingerly, Pat walked toward the river. "This thing is disgusting," he called over his shoulder as they both made their way down the incline.

"I sure hope this is it," Kate said as they reached the shore.

Frankie had been cautiously following along in their wake. He wasn't sure what was going on or what to do about it. Why did Pat answer to the name Abernathy? It sounded like he knew Kate far better than he'd let on. Some part of Frankie needed to see how this played out.

Pat swished the saddlebag in the river, then struggled with the leather ties, finally producing a knife to cut them. They both knelt on the shore as he withdrew a bag that looked exactly like those Frankie's father had taken from the bank decades before. Laying that on the ground between them, Pat sliced it open and they both gasped.

Even from where Frankie stood, the sparkle and glitter of gems flashed brilliantly in the sun. Pat laughed as he reached into a pocket and withdrew something he unobtrusively moved to hold behind his back. Frankie immediately froze in place. Pat clutched a small gun and to Frankie it looked exactly like the one Jay Thurman had wielded the day before.

It no longer mattered if any of this made sense. He had to get that gun.

Kate lifted an extravagant emerald necklace laced with sapphires and diamonds. She set it against her throat as though wearing it and, despite her flushed face, straggling hair and the smears of dirt on her cheeks, turned into a princess out of an old book. "It's beautiful," she gushed. "There's a bracelet and earrings, too, and a matching tiara." Her brow wrinkled. "But these aren't mine. My grandfather's great-uncle was a diamond merchant, you told me so yourself. What would he be doing with these precious old pieces? They must be worth a king's ransom."

"You're right," Pat said. "They're not yours. They're mine." The gun was in front of him now, pointed at Kate. She dropped the necklace and they both stood up.

Frankie was still close to the bank where overgrowth concealed him. He couldn't see how he could rush Pat without risking Kate's safety. Would he really shoot her?

"I don't understand," Kate repeated. "What about my grandfather's file and the diamond merchant—"

"There was no file. For that matter, there was no diamond merchant, either. I did know your grandfather but he wouldn't have shared an office with me if I were the last man on earth. We hated each other," Pat said. "But I knew he had a wife and I knew she was in trouble. I found out about you and your determination to save her...so I called myself Greg Abernathy and made you an offer I knew you couldn't refuse. I needed someone to look around and figured if I gave you a good cover story, the blasted Hastings wouldn't suspect you."

"But why?"

"Simple. I'm sick of barely scraping by. I lost my pension in a divorce…it doesn't matter. While researching this documentary, I came across a letter written by a woman a long, long time ago. It revealed the theft of priceless jewels that had never been disclosed. A man with ties to the Dalton family had it. I, ah, took it."

"You killed Dave Dalton," she said, horrified.

"It had to be done. Just like this has to be done."

"They'll figure out—"

"That I killed you, too? That I killed Jay Thurman before he could shoot his ugly mouth off about who hired him, who gave him a gun, who told him to make as big a distraction as possible just like I've got those clowns doing up at Ten Cent Creek right this minute? The truth is no one knows where the gold went. It was probably discovered and moved decades ago." He'd worked himself up a little as he talked, and now he lowered his voice. "Possibly someone will figure out what I've done, but by then I'll be in Mexico living off an empress's jewels."

"But—"

"Show-and-tell is over," he said jabbing the gun against her ribs. "I'll make it fast—"

Frankie knew it was now or never. He grabbed his key ring out of his pocket and threw it at the rocks on the bank to his left. As both Kate and

Pat looked toward the sound, he took off at a dead run, Pat his target, seeing him through a haze of anger and hate, desperate to stop the man who had manipulated them all in order to line his own pockets. He saw Kate grab Pat's arm and heard gunfire. He registered the fact Kate was on the ground a millisecond before he barreled into Pat.

The impact knocked Pat into the water. Frankie went after him. Pat fired the gun again. Frankie ducked the shot as the older man plowed farther out in the river. Frankie followed. Both of them slipped, but Pat recovered and flung himself away. Frankie grabbed him around the waist and that propelled them both into deeper water. As they struggled, the current caught them and before Frankie could prevent it, they were both swept downstream.

He hung on to Pat, fighting to get the gun as the shore whizzed past. Within a minute, they passed under the bridge. So busy trying not to get shot, Frankie couldn't swim to calmer water. Pat threw his gun hand at Frankie's face and the cold metal hit his cheekbone. He grabbed at the gun right as Pat pulled the trigger. The gun fired and Pat's eyes grew round. Blood spurted into the water from a wound in his throat. Frankie supported his head to keep his face out of the water and began paddling toward shore. By the time he got to a point where his feet touched bottom, he was pretty sure Pat was dead but he dragged him out of the water anyway, dropped his shoulders onto the beach and made sure he wasn't breathing.

He wasn't positive one of Pat's earlier shots hadn't hit Kate. He took a deep breath and began the climb to the road where he'd parked his truck to spy on Kate a lifetime ago. As he stepped onto the road, he found his own truck hurtling toward him.

Kate sat behind the wheel and for a second, their gazes connected through the dusty windshield. She jumped out of the truck and ran to him. "You're hurt," she cried.

"I'm not hurt," he said looking down at himself. His wet shirt was streaked with red. "It's Pat's blood." He put his arms around her. "Are you okay?"

"Shaky, but yes, I'm okay."

"And the baby?"

"Still here," she said.

"Incredible," he whispered.

"What made you come looking for me?" she asked, staring into his eyes. This time he didn't look away.

"I needed to see you," he said, unable to take his arms from around her waist. "I needed to ask you to forgive me."

"For what? For being offended I lied to you? For making you feel used?" Her lips trembled and tears rolled down her cheeks. "For hurting you?"

"For judging you," he said. "For forgetting that I love you and that means I trust you and believe in you without reservation."

"You love me?" she whispered.

"More than life itself," he responded and without further delay pulled her into an embrace that would last a lifetime.

Epilogue

The letter was old and faded but legible, the writing feminine. It was found with Pat Lowell's things and was dated 1965.

"'If you are reading this letter, then you have found the coins I have been hiding for fifty years,'" it began. "'My legal name is Mary Dalton, but I will always think of myself as Mamie Covey. I have loved only one man in my life and his name was William Adler.

The time for excuses is long over. When I was nineteen, my father, who ran the Green Peak Mine in Falls Bluff, promised my hand to an emotionless, widowed attorney named Matthew Dalton. Father ignored my tears; he did not care that my heart and the baby I secretly carried belonged to William.

We wanted to run away but William was young and poor. The answer to our problem came when my father foolishly revealed that a

sizeable gold shipment was coming to the bank.
I talked my William into robbing it. He enlisted
the help of the Bates brothers. I dressed up as a
man. William cracked the safe within minutes.
He and I went into the vault. Earl and Sammy
stood guard. When we'd given them as much
as they could carry, they left the bank. William
and I went back inside. That's when I opened a
drawer and gulped.

There was a woman staying at the hotel where
I worked. I'd met her once or twice and she
struck me with her low manner. I had heard she
was once the mistress of an emperor and that
when he grew tired of her, she stole his wife's
priceless jewels before fleeing the country.

Those jewels were in the vault! I stuffed them
into a bank bag. William cautioned me to not
tell Sammy or Earl. When we left town, we
each had two bags. The men's carried just gold.
One of mine also carried the jewels. We split up
when we got outside town. William and I went
to the spot beside the river where a house had
burned down a dozen years before. There is a
bend in the river where a large boulder we call
the bonnet rock divides the water's flow. We
have named it snag hollow because of a tree…
it is our spot. William hid the jewels along with
my male clothing.

I dressed as a woman again. William left to

join the others taking the full bag of my gold with him to ease my load. I went back to my bed and hid what gold I still had. I waited for word from William until the news spread about what the posse had done. I rode out to see and there was William and the others... I cannot say any more about this; it is too painful.

My father was suspicious of me. He insisted I marry Matthew Dalton. I said I would on the condition we leave this town. Seven months later, I gave birth to William's daughter, Amelia, who Matthew thought was his own child. He was not as successful as he led my father to believe yet I was never tempted to use a single coin. Matthew died young.

The cursed gold remains untouched. If I knew how to repay it, I would. I am old now, my daughter is gone, her daughter is with child. I live with my stepson George and his family in the same house we bought when coming here. He knows nothing of this gold. It is hidden and hopefully remains that way for eternity.

I yearn only to see my beloved again whether in heaven or in hell.

Mamie.'"

"The fourth man was a woman," Kate said when they'd finished reading the letter.

"My great-great-grandmother," Frankie said. "No wonder that town always spoke to me." He kissed Kate's forehead. "Dave Dalton's father was Mamie's stepson so Dave and I weren't related by blood. Dave's father found the coins late in his life and spent them sparingly, passing them on to Dave when he died five years ago. I've talked with Sara who still hasn't found them. My guess is they'll turn up with Pat's belongings. Dave signed his death warrant when he showed that letter to Pat."

"He signed a lot of death warrants that day," Kate said.

Three months later

"GRAM IS DOING GREAT," Kate said as she handed Sierra back her cell phone. She had to break down and get her own. Finding one that worked both in Seattle and here was tricky; in a few weeks, that wouldn't be an issue. "Every time I tell her about the ranch and Frankie, she just beams. She can't remember any of it thirty seconds later, but they're a good thirty seconds every single time."

"Frankie said you sold her house," Sierra said.

Kate nodded. "They're going to tear it down and build a condo. In a way it's sad but Gram couldn't even remember the place when I took her there the last time. I'm moving her to a really nice facility in Falls Bluff in a couple of weeks so I can help Frankie build our new house."

Sierra spontaneously hugged Kate. Pike had been right. She and his auburn-haired girlfriend had formed a fast friendship. Kate was so glad Sierra had taken on a partner so she could spend more time on the ranch.

They were sitting outside on the porch bench and tucked their feet out of the way as Gary, Frankie and their cameraman, Oliver, came out of the house.

"Then all that's left is postproduction work," Gary was saying but Oliver shook his head.

"No, there's one more thing. Frankie had an idea and I think it's great. We're going to burn down the hanging tree."

Gary glanced at Frankie. "Why am I just hearing about it?"

Frankie took Kate's hand and pulled her to her feet where he put both arms around her and looked at Gary from over her head. "Because we just thought of it," he said.

It was nice of him to share the credit, Kate thought, but unnecessary. Still she thoroughly agreed with him. The ghost town would be razed in the fall—it was time for the tree to go, too. Not only was it very old, but it stood only for misery.

That's how it came to be that a week later,

the entire Hastings family gathered on the plateau. Grace held her newest grandson and sat next to Kinsey and Gerard in a beach chair located a safe distance from the tree. Charlie had dug marshmallows out of his backpack and now pestered Chance to carve a stick so he could roast them once the fire got going. Lily and Chance produced chilled cider and paper cups, announcing they were going to make today their combined prenuptial bachelor parties for their wedding next week. Sierra and Pike sat on the tail of his truck, holding hands, smiling at each other, Sierra's diamond sparkling at the base of her throat. She was going to make a fabulous bride come spring, which left just enough time for Kate and Frankie to sneak in a Christmas wedding and welcome a Valentine baby.

As soon as Harry showed up in the tank truck with water to control the blaze, they started the fire. It was an indication of the tree's advanced age and hidden rot that it burned with a vengeance. Kate looked up at Frankie and he smiled at her as he looped his arm around her shoulders.

"I love you," he said close to her ear, "but I swear, sometimes I forget Earl and Samuel Bates weren't your real relatives. I was standing here thinking that we're giving them a Viking send-off."

"Along with one for your great-great-grand-father, William Adler," Kate said. "May he and Mamie rest in peace."

"Well said."

The tree burned for hours and other than spraying the dry grass around its perimeter, needed no intervention. People began wandering off after a while, but not Frankie or the documentary film crew. Nor Kate. There was nowhere in the world she wanted to be but right where she was.

As it burned deep into the ground, something caught Oliver's eye through the camera lens and he called everyone over. They moved as close as they dared.

The truth hit them all at the same moment.

There, under the tree used to punish the thieves, deep down in the roots themselves, lay the plundered coins. They watched as the intense heat reduced them to a lake of molten gold.

"I'll be damned," Frankie whispered.

* * * * *

LARGER-PRINT
BOOKS!

❖HARLEQUIN

Presents®

GET 2 FREE LARGER-PRINT
NOVELS PLUS 2 FREE GIFTS!

LARGER-PRINT BOOKS!
GET 2 FREE LARGER-PRINT NOVELS PLUS
2 FREE GIFTS!

H HARLEQUIN®

Romance

From the Heart, For the Heart

YES! Please send me 2 FREE LARGER-PRINT Harlequin® Romance novels and my 2 FREE gifts (gifts are worth about $10). After receiving them, if I don't wish to receive any more books, I can return the shipping statement marked "cancel." If I don't cancel, I will receive 4 brand-new novels every month and be billed just $5.09 per book in the U.S. or $5.49 per book in Canada. That's a savings of at least 15% off the cover price! It's quite a bargain! Shipping and handling is just 50¢ per book in the U.S. and 75¢ per book in Canada.* I understand that accepting the 2 free books and gifts places me under no obligation to buy anything. I can always return a shipment and cancel at any time. Even if I never buy another book, the two free books and gifts are mine to keep forever.

119/319 HDN GHWC

Name	(PLEASE PRINT)	
Address		Apt. #
City	State/Prov.	Zip/Postal Code

Signature (if under 18, a parent or guardian must sign)

Mail to the Reader Service:
IN U.S.A.: P.O. Box 1867, Buffalo, NY 14240-1867
IN CANADA: P.O. Box 609, Fort Erie, Ontario L2A 5X3

Want to try two free books from another line?
Call 1-800-873-8635 or visit www.ReaderService.com.

* Terms and prices subject to change without notice. Prices do not include applicable taxes. Sales tax applicable in N.Y. Canadian residents will be charged applicable taxes. Offer not valid in Quebec. This offer is limited to one order per household. Not valid for current subscribers to Harlequin Romance Larger-Print books. All orders subject to credit approval. Credit or debit balances in a customer's account(s) may be offset by any other outstanding balance owed by or to the customer. Please allow 4 to 6 weeks for delivery. Offer available while quantities last.

Your Privacy—The Reader Service is committed to protecting your privacy. Our Privacy Policy is available online at www.ReaderService.com or upon request from the Reader Service.

We make a portion of our mailing list available to reputable third parties that offer products we believe may interest you. If you prefer that we not exchange your name with third parties, or if you wish to clarify or modify your communication preferences, please visit us at www.ReaderService.com/consumerschoice or write to us at Reader Service Preference Service, P.O. Box 9062, Buffalo, NY 14240-9062. Include your complete name and address.

HRLP15

LARGER-PRINT BOOKS!
GET 2 FREE LARGER-PRINT NOVELS PLUS
2 FREE GIFTS!

HARLEQUIN®

super romance®

More Story...More Romance

HSRLP15

WESTERN WP PROMISES

YES! Please send me **The Western Promises Collection** in Larger Print. This collection begins with 3 FREE books and 2 FREE gifts (gifts valued at approx. $14.00 retail) in the first shipment, along with the other first 4 books from the collection! If I do not cancel, I will receive 8 monthly shipments until I have the entire 51-book Western Promises collection. I will receive 2 or 3 FREE books in each shipment and I will pay just $4.99 US/ $5.89 CDN for each of the other four books in each shipment, plus $2.99 for shipping and handling per shipment. *If I decide to keep the entire collection, I'll have paid for only 32 books, because 19 books are FREE! I understand that accepting the 3 free books and gifts places me under no obligation to buy anything. I can always return a shipment and cancel at any time. My free books and gifts are mine to keep no matter what I decide.

272 HCN 3070 472 HCN 3070

Name _____ (PLEASE PRINT)

Address _____ Apt. #

City _____ State/Prov. _____ Zip/Postal Code

Signature (if under 18, a parent or guardian must sign)

Mail to the **Reader Service:**
IN U.S.A.: P.O. Box 1867, Buffalo, NY 14240-1867
IN CANADA: P.O. Box 609, Fort Erie, Ontario L2A 5X3

WPBPA16R